PUFFIN STORY BOOKS

Edited by Eleanor Graham

PS 104

SAVAGE GOLD

This is an unusual and magnificent story of adventure, in which young Robert Brown went out to join his father, an anthropologist, roughly a thousand miles from Mombasa. Before he had left the ship which had brought him from England, Robert had encountered two sinister men, one thin and dark, the other round and elephantine, each describing the other as *the most dangerous man in Africa*. Robert was kidnapped at Mombasa, was rescued and continued the journey to Makala, where his father awaited him, but only there did his adventures really begin.

The two mysterious men are tremendous characters, and prove fantastically dangerous opponents. The whole action, in which Robert and his father are vitally involved, has an urgent feeling of deadly intention and actual peril. Kenya is the background of the fast, thrilling story, and the descriptions of scene and life are brilliantly sharp and clear. It is a book for the eager reader, even boys and girls as young as eleven or twelve, but it can be read with equal satisfaction by young and adult.

The Attack

SAVAGE GOLD

A STORY OF ADVENTURE BY
Roy Fuller

WITH ILLUSTRATIONS BY
Robert Medley

PENGUIN BOOKS

Penguin Books Ltd, Harmondsworth, Middlesex
U.S.A.: Penguin Books Inc., 3300 Clipper Mill Road, Baltimore 11, Md
AUSTRALIA: Penguin Books Pty Ltd, 762 Whitehorse Road,
Mitcham, Victoria

—

First published by John Lehmann in 1946
Published in Puffin Story Books 1957

Made and printed in Great Britain
by The Whitefriars Press Ltd
London and Tonbridge

CONTENTS

TO JOHNNY

Darling, in the following story
The only real things are the imaginary
— Except the unimaginably lovely
Country of Kenya used for scenery.
I wish that you could live for ever
In wars so real, beside such unreal rivers.

Chapter I

THE VOYAGE

I

BETWEEN Alexandria and Mombasa two of the ship's passengers particularly impressed themselves on Robert Brown. They were both very much unlike the knitting women, the sleeping old men, the shrieking little girls in white satin, who made up the rest of the first-class passengers. They were called, Robert found out, Count Curnow and Dr Maine.

At dinner, as they were steaming out of Alexandria, Count Curnow (who had just come aboard) was shown by the steward to Robert's table. He was a man of immense fatness and complete baldness; a monocle was wedged in the folds of flesh which surrounded his little black eyes; he wore a grey linen suit that hung loosely on him like the skin of an elephant. Robert stared in fascination as he lowered himself into a chair.

'Good evening, my dear sir,' said the Count.

Robert blushed and shifted about uneasily: when one is

called 'sir' at the age of twelve one is certainly being made fun of.

But the Count gravely directed his eyes to Robert's plate.

'Can you recommend the soup?' he asked.

'Rather over-seasoned,' said Robert.

'Delicious!' said the Count. A great and charming smile spread over his face: the monocle was nearly hidden by fat. 'When you have lived as long in the tropics as I, you will find that no dish can be too highly seasoned. Indeed,' he went on, 'let us have some cayenne pepper brought, for I see none on the table.'

When the soup had been disposed of and before the fish had arrived, the Count said: 'Since we shall be eating together for some time, perhaps I had better introduce myself. I am Count Hugo Curnow. I go as far as Mombasa.'

'My name's Robert Brown. I'm going to Mombasa, too.'

'Splendid,' said the Count. 'I hope we shall see much of each other. Frankly,' he continued, leaning (so far as his stomach allowed him) towards Robert confidentially, 'I regard you as my social salvation on this voyage, for I simply cannot endure these dried-up, horribly polite civil servants and awful talkative missionaries.' He squeezed a little moon of lemon on his fish. 'Just look round. It is like being in a morgue.'

Robert giggled. He found it charming to be treated by Count Curnow as an equal.

'I hope you won't think me rude,' said the Count, as, next day, they were sitting side by side on the boat deck, 'but are you travelling to Mombasa absolutely alone?'

Robert said he was.

'Rather an adventure, isn't it?'

'I thought it was when I started off from England, but I'm getting used to it now. I'm even a bit bored.'

'Tut, tut,' said the Count, with his high-pitched titter. 'A voyage to Africa at your age and bored!'

'Well,' remarked Robert, 'I think Africa is no more exciting than Surrey, and a sea voyage no more an adventure than a bus journey. Look.' And he waved his hand at the fresh

paint and polished brass of the ship, the dozing travellers with their mouths wide open, the cloudless sky and the blue of the calm sea.

The Count tittered again delightedly. The next moment the smile vanished from his face. A line appeared on his great forehead between the now serious eyes.

'You say there is no adventure, no excitement, my dear friend,' pronounced the Count. 'Do you see that man walking by the rail there?'

Robert followed the Count's glance and saw coming towards them the figure of a man; on this ship, in this heat, fantastic in the extreme. He was of middle height, very thin, and tripped along with his hands clasped behind his back. On his head he wore a black hat which was half bowler, half top-hat; his suit was unseasonably and astonishingly black; he wore a pair of spectacles with lenses so dark that they seemed black, too. A white beak of a nose went before him. Two or three books and periodicals were stuffed under each arm.

Robert felt inclined to laugh. The Count must have sensed that inclination for he said in a whisper, close to Robert's ear: 'Yes, he looks harmless enough, even amusing.'

'Who is he?' asked Robert. He spoke in a whisper, too, because the stranger was now passing them, not three yards away.

'The most dangerous man in Africa,' said the Count.

II

For several days Robert saw nothing of Dr Maine (for that was the name of the man in black), but he saw much of Count Hugo Curnow. They were now in the Red Sea and the weather was stifling. During the day-time Robert did little more than lounge in a deck-chair at the Count's side and drink the long cooling drinks which the Count arranged should come to them frequently.

'The solid figure with the greatest surface area,' the Count remarked, 'is the sphere – as you know, my dear Robert. To that figure my own most nearly approximates. Consequently

I perspire to an abnormal degree. So I have always to be replacing the fluid I lose.'

One day the Count idly asked him the purpose of his journey.

'Why, I'm going to join my father,' said Robert.

'In Mombasa?' asked the Count.

'Oh no,' said Robert, 'in Makala – if you know where that is.'

'Makala, Makala,' said the Count to himself.

'It's nearly a thousand miles inland.'

'I believe I have heard of it,' said the Count. 'Your father is perhaps the District Commissioner?'

'No,' said Robert, 'he's an anthropologist.' Then Robert told the Count why he was travelling.

'My mother is dead. My father has been in Africa for two years, living for a lot of the time with a tribe of natives not far from Makala. He's investigating how they live, their habits and religion and songs and so on – that's what an anthropologist does, you know. I was at school in England all this time. It was pretty awful: I had to spend most of the holidays with the headmaster and his ghastly family. And then, just as another dreadful holiday was starting, the head got a letter from my father saying that as it was turning out he was likely to be in Africa for a long time, and that there was a decent English school not too far from Makala, and that he wanted me to go out to him. So you see – here I am. I had a letter from my father, too, but he didn't say very much except that he wanted me to be with him since he had to stay in Africa so long, and that he thought I'd like being in Makala.'

The Count showed interest. But he did not, in return, tell Robert his own purpose in journeying to Mombasa. 'As for me,' he said, 'I am a plain unromantic business man.' He said nothing else. Nor, more provokingly, would he tell Robert anything about Dr Maine.

'*Why* is he the most dangerous man in Africa?' he repeated, when Robert asked him. 'My dear friend, you must know already that there is much evil in the world, but of the *kinds* of evil and the *extent* of evil you can, at your age, have no conception.'

'But –' said Robert.

'Enough, dear boy. Avoid Dr Maine. Avoid him. Should you ever have to choose between advancing towards a charging buffalo and advancing towards Dr Maine, choose, for your safety, the buffalo.'

Dr Maine's black figure was not often visible on deck, and he took, it seemed, his meals in his cabin. They had now passed Aden and the ship was plunging gently in the light seas. The nights with their few but brilliant stars, an electric moon on its back, and the dramatic smoke-black clouds very high and big, were impressive. On one of them, Robert was leaning over the rail, watching the sea cut by the ship's great side into strips of phosphorescence, and listening to the constant hissing of the passing water. It was lateish: no one was about. He was deep in thought, trying to picture Makala and what his life would be there – just as he had tried, before he started off from school, to picture this journey. It was hopeless, he knew, to try to get a glimpse of such future scenes and his life among them (but he still persisted) – how could he, he thought, have imagined the peculiar circular motion of the ship's mast against the fuming sky, or the thin, brown, dried-up lascars of the crew, or the taste of fresh dates, or Count Curnow – or Dr Maine?

He lifted his eyes from the waves, and turned and leaned his back against the rail. At that moment he saw a darker shape detach itself from the dark shape of the winches at the end of the deck. Against the subdued glow of the sky he saw what was the outline of neither a bowler hat nor a top-hat, but partaking of both. A sick throb went through his stomach.

'Dr Maine!' he gasped, involuntarily.

The voice that came to him from a few yards away, through the gloom, was precise and high-pitched. 'Forgive me,' it said, 'if I have startled you. But I have something very important to tell you, and I cannot –'

Robert then saw the peculiar hat fly into the air, and, at the same moment, heard the unmistakable bang of a revolver shot. The shape of Dr Maine disappeared. Some light steps came running along the deck. Robert turned, half-frightened, to meet them; uncertain whether or not to run away. The bulk of Count Curnow loomed up, moving at a pace Robert would not have thought possible.

'What is going on, my dear Robert?' wheezed the Count. 'Are you safe?'

'Yes, quite safe,' said Robert. 'Someone fired a shot at Dr Maine and knocked his hat off.'

'Dear me,' said the Count. 'Did you see who it was?'

'No.'

'Some fellow member of the criminal underworld, no doubt, whom Dr Maine has displeased. Did Dr Maine speak to you?'

'Only a few words – I don't know what he meant.'

'How very mysterious!' said the Count, taking out a large handkerchief and wiping his glistening face. 'What can it all be about?'

Robert observed that the Count's side pocket was still extremely bulky even when the handkerchief had been removed. He walked a few steps and picked up Dr Maine's hat. Through the high, oddly-shaped crown were two holes.

III

On the Count's advice, no report of the incident was made to the ship's officers. To the few passengers who heard the shot the thing remained almost as great a mystery as to Robert, who knew so many more baffling circumstances. That night, Robert lay in his cabin in the heat, listening to the cool air whistling through the pipe in the bulkhead, his mind a fever of speculations and theories. What 'important' communication had the sinister Dr Maine wished to make to him? Who had shot at Dr Maine? Was it the Count? Why had the person behind the revolver thought it imperative to *shoot* to drive Dr Maine off? Would Dr Maine try again? Would the Count (if it were he) try again on Dr Maine?

Robert got up, had a drink of water, and read two chapters of a boring book (borrowed from the ship's library) by Sir Walter Scott. These at last drove him to sleep.

The next day, the Count, as though to protect him, was quietly but constantly at his side. If, in the dead of night, the most dangerous man in Africa were going to accost him and revolver shots were going to whizz past his head, Robert felt glad of a solid, competent character like the Count to rely on. Robert pestered the Count with questions about the night before; the latter, however, was amiably but firmly silent. To escape the pestering he took Robert to his cabin. There, in a large wicker box, were three lizards of a brilliant and revolting purple, and, on the bed, a somnolent chameleon.

'Do you *always* travel about with them?' asked Robert, in amazement.

'Always,' said the Count, picking up the chameleon, and implanting a delicate kiss on its little prehistoric head. 'This is Carlyle.' He stirred the lizards with an affectionate forefinger. '*Their* names are Frederick the Great, Nietzsche and Wagner. You will soon learn to distinguish them. Frederick is the very large one. Nietzsche is the particularly purple one. Wagner is the most loving.'

Robert stared about the cabin for more evidence of the Count's eccentricity. He saw nothing, however, beyond some paper-backed books in a foreign language, a dressing-gown which would have served as a tarpaulin for a haystack, and, on the writing table, a few lumps of brightly flecked rock.

'What are those?' asked Robert, pointing to the stones.

'Specimens, dear boy. Merely geological specimens.' The Count uttered a little shriek. The chameleon, with painful and pernickety steps, was climbing off the bed. 'Carlyle! You will be trodden underfoot by that oafish steward of ours. Get back at once.' The Count fondly returned the creature to safety. 'Now let us go up on deck and discover whether we can see Mombasa yet.'

IV

Mombasa began to reveal its low red roofs and vivid green vegetation. In the calm water of the harbour they passed a dhow and some frail native skiffs. Robert went below to pack a few last things. What excited him more than the prospect of disembarking was the likelihood of seeing Dr Maine in the process, of perhaps having another encounter with him. Robert, in fact, was unwilling that this taste of adventure, of mystery, should fade – as it certainly would when he had left Mombasa, arrived at Makala, and started the routine of school. School! He shuddered at the thought.

He had the address of a friend of his father's who lived in Mombasa, with whom he was to get in touch on arrival so as to be put safely on the train for Makala. The Count, when he had mentioned this arrangement, pooh-poohed it.

'There is not the slightest need to trouble your father's friend. I myself am staying at the Splendide Hotel in Mombasa. If, when we dock, you are too late to catch the Makala train that day, I shall insist on your being my guest for the night at the Splendide. In any case I shall see you safely on the train.'

Robert jumped at this idea – as being rather more interesting than a night with people who would probably treat him as a small boy and send him to bed early with a glass of milk.

The ship docked: swarms of Negro porters came on board and pounced on the luggage. By the time the formalities of disembarking were over, it was too late for the Makala train. The Count secured a taxi: they were soon being driven madly towards the town by an Indian driver wearing an American-style soft hat and his shirt outside his trousers. The Count sat back, perspiring gently in the great heat, and grinned.

'Well,' he said. 'Did you see Dr Maine leave the boat?'

Robert's head was half out of the window, regarding the strange life in the streets.

'No,' he said. 'I forgot to look.'

Chapter 2

THE HUT

I

THE Splendide Hotel was not splendid. It was a detached, white-washed building, two stories high, in a back street. In the hall were three old grey dogs, with hairless and distended stomachs, which on the entry of Robert and the Count came up panting their bad breaths furiously. From the hall one could see the back door where a few dusty hens shuffled about. A cloud of flies rose from the hotel register as Robert made to sign his name.

But the proprietor, a Greek named Panopoulous, welcomed them with a great show of pomp. The Count he greeted respectfully but warmly as an old friend. He bent his dead white face to Robert with excessive amiability. He clapped his hands and two Negroes in long off-white gowns ran in and began to move the luggage with mock energy and no skill.

'You is from English?' said Mr Panopoulous to Robert.

'Yes, I am,' said Robert, baffled, but answering both the possible questions.

'Thank you,' said Mr Panopoulous. He then began to speak to the Count more fluently in another language. Robert,

16

as he stood rather bewilderedly listening, felt suddenly very tired. The brilliant heat, which at first had seemed exhilarating, had given him a headache. He was fiendishly thirsty. He said to the Count, as they walked up the stairs to their rooms:

'Would you mind if I just had sandwiches and something to drink in my bedroom?'

'You are tired,' said the Count, sympathetically. 'Of course – have your little snack, and then away to bed with you. I will arrange it. You have a long journey tomorrow.'

The sandwiches and a drink of sickly pinkness were brought, in due course, by one of the gowned Negroes, and soon afterwards the Count looked in to say good night.

'All is well,' he said, beaming through his monocle. 'Carlyle is a little restless, but not *too* shaken by that dreadful taxi drive. For myself, I have some business calls to make tonight. Mr Panopoulous has arranged for us to be called at eight tomorrow morning, which will give you an amplitude of time for your train. Sleep well, dear boy.'

II

Robert opened his eyes. In the gloom he saw the mosquito net's ghostly funnel narrowing up to the ceiling. It was stiflingly hot. Something had wakened him. It must be the middle of the night.

There was a knock on his door. He sat up and called 'Come in.' The door opened and the light was switched on. Through the sudden dazzle he made out Mr Panopoulous, standing there smiling, a long cigarette between his lips.

'So apology,' said the hotel proprietor.

Robert drew aside the mosquito net and sat on the edge of the bed. 'What's the matter?'

'The Count send *gari* for your conveniently,' said Mr Panopoulous, slowly.

'*Gari?*' said Robert, bemusedly. The Greek's English was so nearly comprehensible that with a little concentration one really ought to be able to understand it perfectly. '*Gari?*

As his eyes became used to the light he saw that Mr Panopoulous was holding a piece of paper towards him. He took it, opened it, and read the following words:

> The Constitutional Club,
> Mombasa,
> Kenya Colony.

MY DEAR ROBERT,

Forgive this intrusion on your sleep: if it were not necessary, of course, I should not have made it. But I have with me here a man who knows what Dr Maine was about to say to you on the ship. It concerns your father very seriously. This man will not come to see you; indeed, I am keeping him here only by a combination of coercion and South African brandy. I think, though, that it is your filial duty to see him: you should hear at first hand what he has to say. If you agree, dear boy, dress, and come along in the taxi with which I am sending this note.

> Your friend,
> HUGO CURNOW

Robert read this angular, foreign writing twice, the second time with great care. He looked at his watch: it was ten to twelve. He reached for his clothes.

'Is the taxi outside the hotel?' he asked Mr Panopoulous, who was watching him all this time along his smouldering cigarette.

'No,' said the Greek, in an affirmative tone.

Robert sighed, dressed hurriedly, and went downstairs, followed by Mr Panopoulous. In the hall was standing a tall Negro dressed in khaki shorts, a tweed jacket, and a sun-helmet with an ostrich feather in it.

'*Jambo, bwana,*' said the Negro to Robert.

Mr Panopoulous hastened to the door and threw it open, disclosing a large but dilapidated Chevrolet standing in the street. He grinned with the air of a conjuror who has just performed a baffling trick. '*Gari,*' he said. The Negro opened the car's rear door, and Robert got in. The Negro went leisurely to the driver's seat and then, with a ferocious grinding of gears, commenced to drive the Chevrolet away at an insane pace.

The unlighted streets flew by. As the car reduced speed to take the corners, Robert sometimes glimpsed feathery leaves, black against the sky. The Negro nonchalantly drew out and lit a cigarette, permitting, as he did so, the Chevrolet to run for a little while on the pavement instead of the road. After a few minutes when the buildings on either side of the street had disappeared, Robert felt a slight uneasiness. He leaned over and touched the tweed coat.

'How far is the Constitutional Club?'

The Negro turned a grinning face but did not speak. He probably did not know English. The car rushed on, over roads now which were not metalled. Robert bounced on the seat. The headlights shone on cardboard-seeming palm trees. Robert remembered suddenly that he did not know the Count's hand-writing, and therefore could not tell whether the letter from the Constitutional Club were genuine or not. A sick feeling of disaster crept up from his stomach. He touched the Negro again.

'Where are we going?'

The Negro did not even turn his head, but drove, if possible, even faster.

III

When, at last, the car stopped, Robert burst out of the door – to find himself, under the moon, on a desolate grassy promontory, with the light before him liquidly on the sea, and the low roaring of breakers in his ears. The only sign of human existence was a small mud and reed hut to his left hand: through its door a feeble gleam was coming. The driver had also got out of the car and, with a not unkindly arm round his shoulder, was urging him towards the hut.

'This is not the Constitutional Club!' Robert cried.

'No. I am sorry,' replied a voice with a foreign accent. This belonged to a short figure carrying an electric torch, emerging from the hut. The torch shone cruelly into Robert's eyes.

'Where am I, then?' said Robert. He was mad with anger.

'Alas!' said the voice. But before it could finish what it had to say, Robert, on an impulse, broke away from the Negro's encircling arm, and dashed across the uneven ground. He heard the voice cry out sharply in an unfamiliar language. He had gone, stumbling, only a few steps when the Negro, running after, caught hold of him by the wrist, and they both went sprawling on the grass. He heard, with intense irritation, a little giggle of amusement from the Negro, as though it were all a game.

Very soon he was being pushed ignominiously through the doorway of the hut. Inside, the air was hot and still. A hurricane lamp gave out a dull and yellow light which fell on a camp bed, a flimsy card-table and a canvas chair. It fell also on a person who was sitting on the chair, a person with flat features, squat and smiling, still holding the electric torch.

'I am sorry,' said the Chinese again. 'Pray do not be alarmed. The Count has been detained. It was necessary to alter the arrangements.'

This was softly and persuasively spoken (in a curiously modulated voice which broke the English sentences into strange little musical phrases), but it did nothing to dispel Robert's sense of alarm.

'Why have I been brought here?' he demanded.

'To meet Count Hugo Curnow, of course,' said the Chinese with the air of replying kindly to a stupid question.

'When will he be here?' Robert began to think that perhaps he *was* being stupid: that this was some friend of the Count. The Count would bring here the man who knew all about the relationship between his father and Dr Maine. And yet, if the Negro had brought the note straight from the Constitutional Club how could *he* have known of any alteration in the Count's plans? Robert went dizzy with trying to think it all out: he was also extremely tired.

'Presently,' said the Chinese. 'Please to sit down.'

Robert looked round, and, seeing no alternative, sat on the bed.

'Who are you?' he asked, abruptly. He felt like being rude to someone, and the Chinese was the obvious victim.

'C. C. Yang – at your service,' said the Chinese, bowing from the waist. 'I am a great friend of Count Curnow.'

'Oh,' said Robert. Really, he thought, it was all perfectly above-board. He cast a searching look at Mr Yang to reassure himself. The Chinese looked back and gave him a smile. The smile revealed two rows of gold teeth, like the teeth of an obscene idol. Robert suppressed a shudder.

The two then sat without speaking. A swarm of miscellaneous insects was banging round the hurricane lamp: by his head, Robert heard the little ping of dive-bombing mosquitoes. The atmosphere was close and tense. Mr C. C. Yang began to chew sunflower seeds and to spit out the husks, with irritating regularity.

After ten minutes Robert could stand it no more. He got to his feet.

'I'm afraid I can't wait for the Count,' he said, rapidly. 'Don't bother about the car – I'll walk back to Mombasa.' And he darted out of the hut.

Mr Yang made no move. Over the threshold Robert became entangled with the driver of the car who was lying across it, wrapped in a blanket. Once more he found himself on the ground with this individual, who giggled again. There was a short struggle. Robert was soon standing, back in the hut, before Mr Yang.

'I am not allowed to leave, then ?' he shouted.

Mr Yang showed his awful teeth in a gentle smile, and removed the husk of a sunflower seed from his dirty white jacket. 'Alas, no,' he said.

Robert then threw himself on Mr Yang with such violence that the canvas chair toppled over and precipitated both of them on the mud floor. The Negro joined them, laughing to himself. Mr Yang was not, however, laughing, and in the mêlée Robert became conscious of a highly unpleasant pressure on his wrist which made him struggle to his feet and bend over backwards in an attempt to relieve the pain.

'You're breaking my arm!' he cried. For the first time in this lonely place, with these two men of different nationality, different lives, he felt frightened.

'I shall break your neck, little boy, if you do not behave yourself,' said Mr Yang, in his tinkling voice.

IV

When Mr Yang had tied Robert up, the Negro laid him on the camp bed. It was only then, as he stared up at the straw underside of the roof, and heard the distant hoarseness of the sea, that Robert realized fully what had happened. He had, of course, for some reason which was unknown to him, been kidnapped. Such an unlikely event followed on fairly naturally from having a revolver shot rocket past his ear. Clearly, he was involved in some logical train of happenings which concerned Dr Maine, and, without doubt, his father. They obviously concerned Mr Yang and the Negro driver, too. And were Count Curnow and even Mr Panopoulous part of it all? He tried to divide these people into teams: Robert Brown's XI versus The Rest. Who was on his side? Robert Brown, naturally. His father. The Count. Against him were, self-evidently, Yang and the Negro. And the captain of *their* side was, surely, 'the most dangerous man in Africa'. And perhaps Mr Panopoulous as twelfth man.

Robert sighed. He was tired, but some nervous tension which he felt along his whole body prevented him from sleeping. He saw only too lucidly his next move, which was to escape and join his father who must be warned soon of the enmity of Dr Maine, who must be told even the fragmentary parts of the plot – whatever it was – which Robert knew. But how to escape? He was tied firmly but not painfully. By turning his head he could just see Mr Yang's yellow (and dirty) toes protruding from the straps of his sandals. That the Chinese was not asleep he could tell by observing the sunflower seed husks which descended from time to time to the ground by Mr Yang's feet. The Negro would probably be just outside the hut, and, if he were sleeping, sleeping with one eye open.

Robert strained his ears to try to hear the Negro moving or snoring. But instead he heard a very faint scuffling noise, and then a hard thud, as of a Negro being hit on the head with a sandbag.

He felt a sudden excited hopefulness. Suppose the Count had come to rescue him!

He turned his head cautiously in the direction of Mr Yang. The Chinese had evidently heard nothing: the feet were there, unmoving. Robert turned his head slowly the other way, towards the door. There were two long minutes in which nothing happened. And then a revolver appeared. Robert held his breath.

The revolver was held by a white hand. The hand was followed by an arm, clothed in black. Eventually, in the doorway, the whole stringy body, the white face, the dark glasses, the beaky nose, the (second) preposterous hat, appeared – of Dr Maine! Robert's mouth opened foolishly in amazement.

Dr Maine's fluty and meticulous voice broke into the silence. 'Er – kindly raise both your hands above your head,' he said to the Chinese.

Robert heard Mr Yang take in his breath with a hissing sound. But whatever Yang did with his hands he did not put them up, because immediately the electric torch came whizzing dangerously at Dr Maine.

Dr Maine ducked, and the torch clattered on the mud wall behind where his head had just been. Maine squeezed the trigger of the revolver. The explosion, in the little space of the hut, sounded like that of a six-inch gun. Yang gave another and louder hiss, and fell on the floor.

Dr Maine put the revolver in his pocket, and walked over to the camp bed.

'Are you hurt?' he said to Robert, anxiously.

Robert could only gape still. So far as he was concerned the world was standing on its head. Dr Maine started rapidly to cut the cords that tied Robert's hands and feet.

'But you are – helping me!' Robert burst out at last.

'Why shouldn't I?' said Dr Maine, sawing away with a penknife.

'But –' said Robert.

'I have been trying to help you ever since Alexandria,' said Dr Maine. 'But we have no time for explanations. Although I gave the Negro outside a pretty shrewd blow, he probably has a pretty tough skull. We must be off.'

'Where to ?' stuttered Robert.

'Makala.'

'Makala!'

The last cord was cut, and Robert jumped off the bed only to find that his legs would not hold him up. He fell on the ground like a baby.

'I've got cramp,' he said.

Without more ado, Dr Maine picked him up, and carried him out of the hut.

'Did you kill Mr Yang ?' said Robert, feeling rather foolish in Dr Maine's surprisingly strong arms.

'No. I shot him in the leg.'

They passed the Negro, who was lying on the ground, groaning. Dr Maine had left his car a quarter of a mile from the hut. They stumbled through the dark towards it.

Chapter 3

EXPLANATION IN A TRAIN

I

THE country of East Africa rises quite quickly from the sea, reaching heights of four to six thousand feet. The climate, tropical at the coast, becomes cool on the plateau, and the vegetation changes with it. The interior contains great plains of scrubby thorn trees on which roam herds of wild animals: from the plains protrude forest-covered or bare hills. In places, due to old volcanic action, are immense mountains, whose summits, even under the equatorial sun, are sheeted perpetually with snow.

In the moonlight Dr Maine's car climbed steadily. His aim was to meet with the Makala train at a place called Lion Gap.

It was half past three in the morning: in the cool air blowing through the windows of the car any vestiges of Robert's sleepiness disappeared. From time to time he looked back down the road to see if the Chevrolet were following them, but there was nothing except the cloud of dust raised by their own wheels. The headlamps lit continually the ghostly eyes of animals by the roadside. Dr Maine drove sitting bolt upright, looking, in his black clothes, as though he were driving a hearse. Robert felt suddenly shy of him.

Dr Maine, with one hand, took off his glasses, and threw Robert a kindly glance. 'I am afraid that you will have to revise your opinion of Count Curnow.'

'He didn't send you?' said Robert.

'No. In fact, it was he who arranged that you should be kidnapped, who sent you the bogus message, who inveigled you into staying at the Splendide Hotel, who shot at me on the ship, who cunningly won your confidence as soon as he came on board at Alexandria, and prevented me from warning you.'

A great light of understanding poured into Robert's mind. 'But who is he?'

Dr Maine gave a deprecatory little cough. 'The most dangerous man,' he said, 'in Africa.'

Robert could not help giggling.

II

It was not until they were in the train, each drinking, after breakfast, his third cup of coffee, that Dr Maine began to enlighten Robert about the curious set of circumstances in which they all found themselves. They had had two hours of uncomfortable but refreshing sleep in the car, waiting for the train at Lion Gap. The sun was already high in the intensely blue sky, the horizon packed with still and towering clouds. The train rushed over the plain.

In the dining car the Negro stewards, in long white gowns, fez, and red embroidered waistcoats, padded about on bare feet.

'I am the representative of the African Gold Company,' said Dr Maine. 'Our headquarters are in South Africa, but for some years we have been interested in the possibilities of mining for gold in East Africa. Gold deposits do exist there, but in country which has been little explored, which is badly served by roads and railways, and where, therefore, the opening up of mines would be a difficult and expensive affair.

'What was necessary, in order to attract my Company, was the discovery of veins of gold so massive that their unearthing would repay, beyond all doubt, the money we would have to spend on providing transport systems, labour and houses – all the items which are indispensable before gold can be mined. Do you understand?'

Robert nodded.

'Your father, Robert,' said Dr Maine, 'made such a discovery.'

He lit a fresh cigarette, and took a delicate puff at it.

'As you probably know,' he went on, 'your father has been living among a tribe of natives called the Wazamba. Although their country is less than a hundred miles from Makala, little is known of them. It is fairly hard to get at, for one thing. In his journeys about it your father discovered ore which he suspected might contain a percentage of gold. Travellers in the Wazamba country in the past had brought back similar reports, but apparently no one had taken the trouble to investigate them. It so happened that I was in Makala – on leave, on a shooting expedition – when your father returned there after his first visit to the Wazambas. We met at the house of Mr Craig, the District Commissioner. As soon as I saw your father's specimens I was interested. They proved to be samples of first-class gold-bearing ore. I went back to my Company after my holiday, and persuaded them to send a small expedition to East Africa to find out the extent of the gold deposits in the Wazamba country.

'They were, it turned out, very considerable. So considerable that my Company decided it would be profitable, despite all the difficulties, to work them. And then the trouble began. Two kinds of trouble.

'The first was this. It had been impossible to keep the expedition to East Africa a complete secret, though we had done our best. It came to the knowledge of another gold-mining company, the Consolidated Mining Company. Of course, they did not know the whole story: they did not know your father, or where the gold was, or how much there was of it. But they were determined to find out, and for that purpose they employed Count Hugo Curnow. Curnow is known not only in South Africa, but in the United States, in Mexico, in Persia, in China. He is a strange product of our modern world. With a very few exceptions, all the products of the earth, and all the things we make out of them, are controlled by great commercial companies. On the surface, these companies conduct their affairs in an orderly manner – their employees work, their directors have meetings, the accounts of the companies are published, and show a profit or a loss. But behind the scenes many companies, in their efforts to get business, in order to sell more of their goods, to conquer their rivals, use violent and illegal methods. They use men like Curnow. And Curnow uses men like Yang.

'Well, Curnow proceeded to find out all he could – by investigation, by bribery, by intelligent guesswork. He found out the major difficulty of the whole project, and that is where the second kind of trouble began.'

Dr Maine eyed Robert sharply. 'Are you sure that you understand what I'm talking about?' he demanded.

Robert was not quite sure, and during Dr Maine's long speech his attention had been a little diverted to the scenery outside the carriage window, but he said, promptly: 'Yes.'

'This was it,' Dr Maine went on. 'Although the Wazamba country is in territory which is nominally under British control, that control has never been exercised very much, for several reasons. For one thing, the Wazamba, until recently, were a warlike tribe, and to avoid any possible trouble the British have never interfered with it. For another thing, the country, as I have said, is pretty difficult to get at. For a third thing, there is little British – or any – trade with the Wazambas and no British settlers, so the British Government is not interested.

'The result is, the Wazamba country is still effectively ruled by its king, and the British Government would have to have very strong reasons indeed to upset any of his decisions.

When we sounded the British authorities with regard to a possible concession over the gold-bearing part of the Wazamba country they simply said, more or less, that it was up to the Wazamba king.

'Now this was very awkward, because the king regards with suspicion all Europeans. In the first place, it would prove very difficult to negotiate with him at all; and, in the second place, once he knew that the result of a concession would be to have scores of white men in his country, negotiations would be pretty sure to break down.

'Luckily, his dislike of white men has one exception, and that is your father. Your father has won the king's confidence – after much hard work. Your father is just about the only white man who knows the language and the people.

'Naturally, my Company wanted to engage him as negotiator, and, if he was successful in getting us a concession, as adviser to the Company on native problems. This would not prevent him going on with his anthropological researches. On the contrary, it would enable him to continue them long after the money provided by the learned society, which at first commissioned them, was exhausted. Your father agreed to the proposition, and, since it looked as though he would be in East Africa for a long time, sent for you.

'Are things becoming clearer to you now, Robert?'

'Yes, they are,' said Robert, eagerly. 'I suppose I was kidnapped by the Count so that by holding on to me he could force my father to stop working for your Company and work for his.'

Dr Maine stubbed out his cigarette. 'Very succinctly put. That was precisely it.'

Chapter 4

MAKALA

I

THE rest of their journey was without incident. At lunch-time the next day they changed to the comic branch-line railway which went to Moru, within twenty miles of Makala, and which accommodated the third-class passengers in unroofed carriages. At Moru they hired a car to take them straight to Mr Craig's house at Makala, and there Robert at last met his father.

Major Richard Brown was a thick-set man in his fifties, his skin dark through a lifetime in sunny climates, his manner shy and undemonstrative. He shook Robert's hand as though his son had just come back from a week-end in the country. But when Robert and Maine told him of the adventure at Mombasa, he began to pace up and down the room in a way that, for him, was very emotionally agitated.

'Clearly,' he said, when he had heard it all, 'until the concession is obtained from the Wazambas, you must never be left alone, Robert.'

against their being inveigled into any house or conveyance, particularly by a Chinese or a particularly fat man.

'Do you really think,' said Robert to his father, 'that the Count or Yang would follow me here?'

'I don't know,' said the Major, 'but I am not taking any risks. I think I ought to tell you, Robert, that personally I am very much opposed to gold being mined at all in the Wazamba country. As soon as the industry starts, the elaborate, and, on the whole, satisfactory social system of the Wazambas – which has existed almost unchanged for centuries – will be destroyed. All the disadvantages of European civilization will be introduced, without any of the advantages. Instead of the taboos of the tribe, the Wazambas will have the taboos of the African Gold Company, and those taboos are chiefly laziness and high wages.'

'Then why are you helping the African Gold Company, Father?'

'Only because I think it will be a more kindly master for the Wazambas than Curnow's Consolidated Mining Company, or, perhaps, any other company which goes into that country to make its fortune. Alas, it is inevitable in the end that the Wazamba gold will be dug out, and better a company to dig it out which employs someone like Maine than a company which employs Curnow.'

'I see,' said Robert.

'And now, of course,' went on the Major, 'after your experiences in Mombasa, Robert, I would be very pleased to see the Consolidated Mining Company utterly defeated.'

'So would I,' said Robert. 'I'd like more than anything for the Count to know that I've seen through him, and think him an utter blackguard. When I think how he pretended to look after me –!'

'I feel rather sympathetic towards the Count,' remarked Charles Craig, who had been listening to all this. 'He seems to be a very able man.'

'I am not capable of such *detachment*,' said Robert, kicking Charles surreptitiously.

33

The town of Makala is not large. There is a stretch of fairly respectable shops along the main road from Moru: there is a small hotel (the one in which Dr Maine was accommodated) not unlike the Splendide in Mombasa: there is the English Club, the few houses of the English civil servants and the block of low wooden administrative buildings. The rest is primitive, and centres round the native market where the population, the flies, and the smells are thickest. Here are more shops, but windowless and doorless – they consist merely of a little room with the street wall missing so that one can see what is for sale in the shop. The native inhabitants of Makala are tall and very black, with dignified and handsome features. The women, for dresses, wind round their bodies lengths of brightly coloured stuff which reach from armpit to ankle, so that, with their stately walk, they look like prima donnas. Makala is three thousand feet above sea level and the temperature is therefore not oppressive, though high. The sun and sky are brilliant. All around rise green-covered hills like inverted basins.

Robert and Charles walked solemnly into town, with William Kapaki a pace or two behind them. Robert wanted to buy shirts and shorts.

'I will take you to Indian Joe's,' said Charles. 'He'll make them for you before you start off next week.'

Outside Indian Joe's shop hung print dresses and leather belts: inside were bottles of bile-coloured brilliantine and cards of buttons. In a corner was a sewing machine, with a Negro treadling away behind it. The floor of the shop was covered with small Indian children, the girls with their hair in little dark plaits like the tails of rodents, the immodest boys in shirts and no trousers. Indian Joe came forward to welcome them.

'Good morning, Mr Craig,' he said. When he spoke he showed, to Robert's horror, tongue and gums stained an unbelievably bright pink with betel nut.

'Now what can I show you?' asked Indian Joe. 'Some nice

sandals, maybe? Or stockings? Very nice stockings from England. Not too expensive. Or I have plenty of combs.'

'No, Joe,' said Charles. 'My friend just wants you to make him some shorts and shirts in khaki drill. He is going on *safari*.'

'Ah,' said Indian Joe. '*Safari*. Well, I am very busy to make things.' His manner was suddenly less amiable.

'Don't be silly, Joe,' said Charles. 'You know you are never too busy to make things for the wretched English. You double your prices for us.'

'Maybe,' said Indian Joe. 'But I am busy all the same. Look, my boy has a nice pile of work.' He waved his hand towards the sewing machine.

The two boys looked in the direction of the hand. They saw the grinning Negro sewing round the enormous waist of a pair of white shorts which would have fitted the hindquarters of a bull.

'My goodness,' said Charles. 'If all your customers are that size you certainly have some work on hand.'

Robert stared at the shorts in fascination. A disconcerting suspicion was growing in his mind. 'Come on,' he said to Charles. 'Joe *is* too busy.' And he walked out of the shop to where William Kapaki was waiting in the street.

Charles came after him. 'I say,' he said, 'you shouldn't have given up so easily. I always have an argument with Joe. He'd probably have made them for you in the end, and for a few bob extra.'

'Those trousers,' whispered Robert. 'Don't you see who they would fit?'

'You mean –'

'Count Curnow.'

'My goodness,' said Charles. 'I wonder whether you're right.'

'I think I am. Did you notice that when you told Indian Joe that I wanted the clothes to go on a journey he quickly said he couldn't make them? He must have twigged who I was.'

'You think he's one of the gang, like Mr Yang?'

'Not necessarily,' said Robert. 'But under the influence of the Count.'

'Who must be in Makala,' exclaimed Charles, 'otherwise Joe couldn't have measured him for the shorts.'

They both looked up and down the street, as though they expected to see the Count's elephantine figure walking along it. But, apart from a few natives sitting on their haunches on the shady side and a rickshaw slowly coming up the hill on the Moru road, it was empty.

'Of course,' said Charles, polishing his glasses, thoughtfully, 'it is ridiculous for Indian Joe – or the Count, if the Count is behind him – to think he can hold up the expedition to the Wazambas simply by refusing to make you some clothes.'

'Perhaps – and I think this is likeliest – Indian Joe, being under the Count's influence, was just too frightened to do anything for me, one of the rival party,' said Robert.

'What is absolutely clear is that the Count has by no means thrown in his hand. And perhaps those shorts of his are for a *safari*, too.'

'What do you mean, Charles? For a journey to the Wazambas? Crikey!'

At that moment the rickshaw passed them. Robert was not paying any particular attention to it, but out of the corner of his eye he saw, protruding from the seat towards the shaft like an enormous rolypoly pudding, a white leg. He clutched Charles' arm.

'Did you see that?'

'Did I see what?' said Charles, putting on his glasses.

'That leg. A man in that rickshaw with his leg in plaster of Paris.'

'Well?' said Charles slowly. 'What about – ?'

And then they both said together: 'Mr Yang!'

In unspoken agreement they moved off after the rickshaw, William Kapaki following them unemotionally as he had long followed the irrational and violent impulses of Europeans. The rickshaw was just breasting the hill, the native between the shafts was walking. Robert and Charles followed warily.

'One of the gang, like Mr Yang. One of the gang, like Mr Yang. The place is alive with the agents of the Consolidated Mining Company,' whispered Charles, melodramatically.

'Of course, it may *not* be Mr Yang,' said Robert.

'I prefer to think that there cannot be *two* men likely to be in Makala with smashed legs,' said Charles. 'One must have some respect for the theory of probability.'

The rickshaw reached the level ground at the top of the hill. The native pulling it broke into a trot. To the uncontrolled delight of the natives squatting in the shadow, Robert and Charles (and, through necessity, the unfortunate William Kapaki) quickened their pace to a half-run and the perspiration began to run down their temples.

'What really are we following it for?' panted Charles.

Robert turned to him a face on which he tried, through the heat, to show irony and contempt. 'To find out where they all are in Makala, of course.'

'If it is not Mr Yang I shall strangle you,' said Charles, wiping his face as he ran.

'Well, you were certain it *was* a minute ago.'

William Kapaki, bewildered but still good-humoured, ran behind them uttering small grunts of protest. They were now leaving the centre of the town, and the rickshaw suddenly turned off the main road into a tree-lined avenue of scattered houses. The boys were about to follow it when William Kapaki put on a spurt and caught them by the arms.

'No, *bwana*,' he said to Charles. 'Not down there.'

'Don't be ridiculous, William. I regard this as a perfectly public, indeed main, street.'

'*Bwana* Brown said no.'

There was some discussion before William uneasily gave way, during which Robert kept an anxious eye on the disappearing rickshaw. At length they all advanced cautiously down the street.

The rickshaw became visible again a few hundred yards away. It was stopped and the occupant was being assisted out of it by the rickshaw boy. Robert, Charles, and William Kapaki stopped, too, and pressed close to the trees which bordered the road. The man with the plaster leg hobbled, on two sticks, out of sight. The rickshaw boy picked up the rickshaw shafts and trotted off. The street was absolutely empty.

The boys and William went slowly on again. Robert had noted carefully the precise spot where the rickshaw had stopped. The houses in the street were few, all detached and set in fairly large gardens. The three came to a footpath leading off the street and apparently round the backs of the houses.

'Let's go down here,' whispered Robert, 'and come upon them from behind.'

'Very well,' said Charles. 'Only let us have no nonsense about " coming upon them". We are here for observation not action.'

William was shaking his black head with foreboding, but followed the boys down the footpath. They emerged, among some beautiful poinsettia trees whose dark green was splashed with crimson blossom, at the back of two houses, into either of which (it seemed to Robert) the man with the plaster leg could have gone. Both the houses were built in a curious style of architecture: mainly corrugated iron and twentieth-century suburban red brick but ornamented with a few small onion-shaped domes and concrete oriental pillars painted blue. The boys peeped cautiously through the trees at the blank windows.

'Which one ?' said Charles.

'Who knows ?' said Robert. 'Watch carefully for a yellow face.'

No yellow, or, indeed, any other colour of face appeared. In the back garden of one of the houses some washing was spread on the bushes. The clucking of hens could be heard. William Kapaki sat down resignedly on his haunches. The escapade began to seem ridiculous and boring.

'Shall we go home ?' said Charles.

'Just a minute,' said Robert, feeling in some way embarrassed and responsible for the lack of action. He walked out of the trees and began to sidle among the bushes which skirted the nearest house, so as to get a view of an open first-floor window – the only window in the side wall.

As, at length, he stood underneath it, merely the lower half of his body hidden in the foliage, a head, to his sudden sickly astonishment, popped out and looked him in the eyes. Despite the lather which half covered it, he recognized it only too easily as belonging to Count Hugo Curnow. The sunlight glinted on his monocle.

'Good morning, my dear boy,' called the Count, waving amiably at him.

'Good morning,' was the only reply the stupefied Robert could make.

'If you will be so kind as to wait until I have finished shaving I will join you in the garden,' went on the Count, with a great smile.

'All right,' said Robert, before he realized that the very last thing he wanted was the Count out here with him.

'And how do you find Makala?' asked the Count, conversationally.

Robert gaped up at the window. What he could hardly grasp, confronting the Count like this, was the turn of events which had changed the agent of the Consolidated Mining Company from a charming companion to a dangerous enemy. Adding to his confusion was the Count's manner, which was just as friendly, intimate, and solicitous as it had been on the ship or in Mombasa. Robert pulled himself together. But he still felt he could not leave the Count abruptly.

'Well, I'm afraid you will have to excuse me,' he called up. 'I must go and buy some shorts and shirts.'

The Count said: 'Oh, I can't let you go away like that.'

Robert correctly read a sinister meaning into these innocent words. He turned and dived into the bushes. As he went he heard Charles' voice:

'Look out, Robert. The Chinaman!' it said.

Robert had a bad moment of panic. His legs felt hampered by more than the long grass, as in a nightmare. He could not find Charles or William Kapaki among the trees. He felt strongly that Yang was advancing on him from behind.

At last he came out on to the path. To the left, Charles and William were looking wildly about them. Beyond, hobbling along on his sticks, was Mr Yang. He had a knife tucked under one arm, like a newspaper.

'Here I am,' Robert shouted, without being able to keep a little catch of relief from his voice.

Charles and William rushed up to him. 'We must get into the street,' said Charles. 'They won't dare to do anything there.'

'Shall I give that man a blow?' asked William Kapaki, indicating Mr Yang.

'No,' said Charles. 'It's awfully willing of you, William, but no. He is not carrying that knife as an ornament.'

They all ran down the path, away from Yang. Where it joined the road a tall Negro was standing, wearing a sun-helmet with an ostrich feather in it. Robert stopped dead.

'That's the native who drove the taxi in Mombasa. We can't get through that way.'

They could now see the street quite plainly. Disconcertingly, life was going on in it in the dullest way. A Negro came past on a bicycle. A small Indian boy carrying a basket looked down the path for an instant. A long-tailed and mangy dog sniffed about.

Robert could hardly restrain himself from calling for help. Again he felt the nightmarish sense that ordinary life had developed a grotesque and dangerous streak from which he could not escape. But he realized that shouting would not do them the slightest good.

'Which way will the Count come?' said Robert. 'He's in the house.'

'That way,' said Charles, pointing to the taxi-driver. 'In any case, I prefer to tackle the Chinese. Although he's got a knife, he's also got a gammy leg.'

They turned round. William picked up a large stone. By this time Yang was only the length of a cricket pitch from them. He was fumbling with the knife. William, with a mighty sweep of his arms, pushed the boys flat into the bushes at the side of the path, and in the same movement hurled the stone straight at Yang's plaster-encased leg. Yang's knife passed the stone in mid-air, and came whistling by William's head.

The boys, with their heads in the grass, heard the crash of breaking plaster and a horrible scream from Mr Yang. William threw himself down beside them.

'Go quickly,' he said.

They went very quickly. After plunging about in the undergrowth, scratching their skin and tearing their clothes, for what seemed to them an unconscionable time, they found themselves in a little ravine over which, a few yards in front of them, went a bridge which carried the main Moru road. In the stream running through the ravine some women were washing clothes. A few Negroes leaned idly over the parapet of the bridge, including a native policeman. They were safe.

'Did I say I felt sympathetic towards the Count?' remarked Charles, picking thorns from his filthy arms.

Chapter 5

THE EXPEDITION

I

IT was clear that Count Hugo Curnow had not changed his tactics; that kidnapping still seemed to him to be a simple way of serving the interests of the Consolidated Mining Company. Major Brown consequently put Makala out of bounds for Robert and Charles, and Mr Craig sent off telegrams trying to put the machinery in motion which would expel the Count and Mr Yang from the country as undesirable aliens. But Mr Craig had no faith that any result could be expected for many weeks. The administration of this part of Africa was lethargic.

William Kapaki was rewarded by the Major for his timely and courageous action against Yang, by the purchase for him (not at Indian Joe's) of a jersey in a singularly violent and repulsive combination of mustards and mauves. Of this he became very proud, and wore it whether the days were cool or hot. William, in spite of a little education at a mission school in Kenya and several years' service as house-boy in European families, was still a very simple young man. His main interests in life appeared to be clothes, food, and a desire to please the Major. His clothes were few but well assorted. On his head he

42

wore chiefly an antique tweed cap with flaps which could be let down to cover the ears, a cap of the type worn on railway journeys by old men in the nineteenth century. The upper part of his body he now covered with the new jersey, but he also had a football shirt in tangerine and green hoops. Normally, he wore khaki shorts, but for special occasions he put on a pair of chef's blue and white check trousers. At such times he wore, too, a pair of brogue shoes in yellow leather, unless he was walking a good deal, in which case he carried them round his neck. He had a thick stick, with the handle shaped like an ostrich's head, and the lobes of his ears had been pierced to admit decorative wooden cylinders three inches in diameter. When he left off the cylinders he tidily looped his lobes over the main part of the ears.

William could roast a piece of beef or grill fish, and even make an omelet, but he had never eaten European food and did not intend to. He lived principally on *posho*, which is a porridge of maize meal, made over the fire in an iron pot, and eaten by dipping the hand into it. After a good blow-out of *posho*, William would smoke with relish a small, thick-stemmed pipe.

Robert and Charles, confined to the house and garden, talked a good deal to William, and got him to play cricket with them. He played with the skill of a child of three, and constantly interrupted the game by collapsing into laughter at his own awkwardness. Waiting for the expedition to start, unable to go into Makala, the boys became bored and therefore a nuisance. Charles, conducting a silly experiment in the shed he used as a laboratory, blew up a retort and precipitated a quantity of sulphuric acid over a new pair of grey flannel trousers. Robert, hitting out wildly at a slow underhand delivery from William, which bounced three times, broke a bedroom window.

Such incidents led to bigger rows than might have been expected, because the Major, Mr Craig, and Dr Maine were all irritable at the unexpected difficulties which had suddenly beset the planning of the expedition.

The Major and Mr Craig were taking their cars – both had

43

large American sedans – and, in addition, it had been decided to hire two cars with box bodies to take the stores. Dr Maine was to drive one of these, and a native or Indian driver hired to drive the other. They had been ordered through the one and only garage in Moru, which was procuring them from Kenya. But the days passed and the cars did not appear. Major Brown interviewed the garage owner, putting on for the occasion his fiercest military manner.

The garage owner was a lean and polite Indian, full of apologies. The accursed agents in Kenya had failed to obtain the cars. He had written them and telegraphed them, but without any result except promises. The Major asked for the agents' telephone number. Alas, the garage owner had never had it, or if he had, had mislaid it. But Major Brown could be assured that all which could be done was being done.

The Major went away very angry indeed, beginning to suspect that here, on a larger and more important scale, an affair was taking place similar to that of Robert's shorts and shirts at Indian Joe's. He drove back to Makala, to Dr Maine's hotel for a conference. In the main street he narrowly missed colliding with two cars with box-bodies, one of them driven by a Negro wearing a sun-helmet with ostrich feathers.

II

Count Curnow not only managed to divert for his own use and to the embarrassment of Major Brown's expedition, the two cars, but also a quantity of food, a primus stove, and three rifles. He obviously had much money at his disposal, and he was using it for bribery and for equipment in the most reckless way. In a way, too, which suggested (like the shorts) that he intended to visit the Wazambas himself: for although by cutting off supplies to Major Brown he could delay, he could not stop, the expedition. If he *did* mean to go, then it looked as though he would be there first, and since he was not going for the purpose of admiring the scenery, the Major and Dr Maine were prepared for trouble.

With some difficulty Major Brown got more food – though

he had to be content with corned beef and plum jam instead of canned chicken and bitter marmalade. Dr Maine succeeded in finding some rifles which had been used in the East African campaign of the 1914–18 war, and Mr Craig made a trip round his farmer friends, fifty miles away in the highlands, and borrowed a Ford light van and an ancient Dodge touring car. A plump native named Joseph was hired to drive the Dodge. He had a fearful squint but seemed sober and competent. Maine hired also an old Negro called Mgambe who had long experience of hunting trips with white men.

So the expedition, with a good deal of creaking, began to take shape. The food, the clothes, the petrol, the tents, the presents for important Wazambas, the cigarettes, the medical supplies, the ammunition, the rifles, were stored away in the cars. Everyone produced a number of personal things of the utmost importance and protested when Major Brown refused to pack them. Robert was allowed a cricket ball, Charles a small microscope, Dr Maine one book, and Mr Craig half a dozen packets of indigestion tablets.

One morning, at eight o'clock, they set off. The order of going was the Major, Robert, and Charles in the first car: Mr Craig, alone, in the second, which was loaded with the more fragile items of equipment: then came Joseph driving the Dodge, with William Kapaki as passenger: and, finally, Dr Maine and Mgambe in the Ford van.

The way to the Wazamba country lay over a high plateau which was reached by narrow and treacherous roads cut out of the banks of the rivers which drained it. Almost as soon as the cars left Makala they began to climb, well spaced out so that the rear vehicles might escape, to some extent, the clouds of red dust thrown up by the wheels from the unmetalled road.

Robert leaned out of the side window to look at the river crawling fifty feet below. The car's off-side wheels were not more than two feet from the unfenced edge of the road. A pulse throbbed in his stomach. Major Brown, his hide-coloured face impassive, drove cautiously but unconcernedly. The car turned successfully round a number of hairpin bends, and avoided nicely the jutting rocks on one side and the precipice on the other. Robert concealed his nervousness and after a while forgot it.

The sky was piercingly blue, and the sheets of vegetation down to the river a soft and brilliant green. Occasionally they came upon walking natives, who, on hearing the cars, scuttled like spiders up the steep roadside and waited, watching, until they had passed. In less precipitous places, little naked boys, holding long sticks, superintended the grazing of diminutive humped cattle, and sucked their fingers in wonder as the expedition left them behind. In the still air, high above the river, buzzards were idly suspended, hardly moving their hairlike wings. The sun rose towards the zenith, and it grew very hot.

About noon, Major Brown made the signal to stop. The cars drove off the track to a flat but rock-strewn space under the shelter of a craggy cliff where a single euphorbia tree pointed up its dull-green candelabra. Before them was now visible part of the huge plain which they had to cross, its dry grass ashen against the plump white clouds fringing the sky at the horizon.

They all got out of the cars, groaning, and stretching their legs like cats. William and Joseph began to prepare lunch. Dr Maine sat on a rock and removed his black hat.

'It is far from being a good road,' he said in his finicky voice.

'It is a long time,' said Mr Craig, 'since my stomach was agitated so vilely. Perhaps I was unwise to eat even one sausage at breakfast time. What is for lunch?'

'Bully beef,' said the Major, 'paw paw, biscuits and cheese, and coffee.'

'Oh dear,' said Mr Craig.

'There are much worse roads in front of us,' continued Major Brown. 'Or, rather, no roads.'

'Would you think me very rude,' remarked Charles, who had been staring meditatively at Dr Maine, 'if I asked you why you wear those rather odd clothes, Dr Maine?'

'My dear Charles!' protested Mr Craig.

'I should think you very rude,' said Dr Maine, putting on his hat. 'And what is more, I shan't tell you.'

'I suppose,' said Charles, 'that it is a way of making a protest against society. Like a poet wearing his hair long.'

'I don't know where you pick up these ideas,' sighed Mr Craig.

'I suppose it is,' said Dr Maine.

'Not a very effective expression,' said Charles.

'On the contrary,' said Dr Maine, 'a *very* effective expression. But an ineffectual *protest*. However, it is very unfair of you, Charles, to probe into adult motives in this way. I think, without flattering myself, that my personality, clothes and all, has a certain effect which people do not usually analyse. Robert thought me once – perhaps still thinks me – a powerful and sinister figure.'

Robert blushed. 'Oh, I don't.'

'When I was a young man,' Dr Maine went on, 'I was far too amiable. I was just as amiable to everyone as I am to you now. No one feared me, and therefore no one had any consideration for me. Everyone, in fact, imposed upon me. I found that I was making no headway at all in the world. Therefore, with one violent gesture, I changed my appearance and my job.'

'And did it work?' inquired Charles.

'Splendidly. Until gradually, even with my disguise, I found myself becoming amiable again – too kind, too confiding, too *nice*.'

'So what did you do?'

'Why, I changed my appearance and job again. And again. And again. Do you see? A little revelation of the nature of my character has occurred just now – I said I shouldn't tell you why I wore these clothes.'

'And are you really a doctor?' Robert asked, boldly.

'Oh, yes,' said Dr Maine, his mouth full of bully beef. 'I am a doctor of music.'

III

In the shadows of the rocks they all dozed for half an hour. They were roused by Major Brown, who, without wishing to exhaust everyone, was anxious to press on so that camp could be pitched for the night at the far side of the plain where water and probably fresh meat from a village could be had. The cars drove on to the road again, in the same order.

The track now descended gently to the plain. On the right the ground fell away more steeply. The cars had hardly gone fifty yards when an alarming sound was heard, as though the height on the left were falling in. What materialized was something less formidable, but formidable enough. A boulder as big as a cabin trunk fell on the bonnet of Mr Craig's car. The noise was tremendous.

The cars stopped. The Major leaped out of his.

'Get under cover!' he shouted.

The whole party squeezed itself against the left-hand side of the road, and there, for five minutes, it stayed. At length, Dr Maine, revolver in hand, crept out and round the Ford van, and peered up at the skyline of the summit which overhung the road. There was nothing except the yellow and brown layers of rock and the scrubby thorn trees and the bright sky. Dr Maine stood up.

'All right, I think,' he said.

'Good Lord, Maine,' said Mr Craig, eyeing the revolver. 'Do you think someone pushed that rock down?'

'I don't know,' said Maine, still gazing up.

'Are you hurt, Craig?' said the Major, anxiously.

Mr Craig, after his terrifying experience, was astonishingly unconcerned. 'Not at all – outwardly, at least,' he added petulantly. 'Since my nerves have obviously sustained a severe shock I tremble to think how my digestion will be affected. Especially after bully beef.'

'I am sorry to have brought you into this,' said Dr Maine.

'I'm not convinced that it was *not* an accident,' said the Major.

William and Mgambe squatted on the road as though

nothing had happened: even Joseph, beyond squinting rather more than usual, did not seem to be alarmed. The boys were very excited.

'A typical Mr Yang trick,' pronounced Robert, without any doubt at all.

'Obviously,' said Charles, 'they aimed for Major Brown's car so as to block the whole expedition – and missed.'

They all went out to examine the damage. Mr Craig's car was beyond repair – by the expedition, at any rate. Its owner looked at it sadly.

'The insurance company will never believe me,' he said. 'What are we to do?'

'Throw it over the ravine,' said Dr Maine, cruelly.

'Throw it over the –' cried Mr Craig. 'Good Lord, Maine, you can't be serious!'

'I'm afraid he is,' said Major Brown. 'The road is too narrow to get the Ford and the Dodge past it: the front axle is gone, and I don't see how we can jack it up on to the rear wheels to tow it. But I've no doubt, my dear Craig, that the African Gold Company will fully compensate you if your insurance company doesn't. Eh, Maine?'

'Of course.'

'Well,' said Mr Craig, dubiously, sliding an indigestion tablet into his mouth. 'I suppose you are right. It seems a dreadful thing to me.'

The whole party (except Dr Maine, who kept watch for any further boulders) got to work: first, on pushing the boulder over the precipice at the side of the track, and then, after unloading it, on the car. The car seemed immovable. William, Joseph, and Mgambe started, as they pushed, to sing over and over again a little musical phrase indicative of pushing, which ended with a ferocious shout marking the moment of greatest effort. Charles and Robert, as they picked up the melody, joined in with sweaty grins. It may well have been this shanty which enabled them at length to poise the car on the edge, and with a final shove send it rolling, like an episode from a film, down the steep slope. It finished up, with a crash that made Mr Craig wince, against a sharp ridge of rock.

49

Room was found for Mr Craig with Joseph in the Dodge. The contents of Mr Craig's car were almost all, somehow, accommodated in the other cars. Everyone had much less room, but, as Dr Maine remarked, they would soon eat their way to comfort again. The expedition drove off.

IV

Almost immediately they were on the plain. It had looked, from the road, level and smoothly grassed, but in reality the parched ground was irregular and the grass mingled with stunted thorn trees which made the going difficult. The only ways across it, neither of them direct, were the dry beds of streams and the narrow paths trodden out by generations of natives which one finds all over Africa. Among the thorns roamed herds of zebra and wildebeest and high-leaping gazelles. Once, they came upon three ostriches which ran away from them at the speed of a train, their necks and bodies carried perfectly still over their racing legs. Whirling, leaning pillars of red dust were whisked by the wind over the plain. The cars bounced and rattled on the cracked earth.

They were well behind schedule. At five o'clock, with the sun going rapidly down the sky, Major Brown made the signal to stop.

They had been following for some time the bed of a tiny river, driving in the bed itself where that was possible, and taking to the level mud of the banks when they came to any pools – green, stagnant pools into which tortoises flopped at the sound of their approach. Where the Major had chosen to stop, the river had encountered and swerved round a spur of rock. The spur was flat on top and commanded, although not high, a pretty wide view of the surrounding plain.

'We can't make the village, I'm afraid, before sunset,' said Major Brown. 'If you all agree, I think we ought to pitch our tents here while it is still light.'

'I suppose so,' said Mr Craig, rubbing his cramped legs. 'That means bully beef again, eh?'

'Yes.'

'Ugh!'

A fire was lit on the tip of the spur, and the tents pitched further back where the rock sank a little beneath the soil, so that the pegs were able to get a purchase. The cars were driven round still further to the rear, making the camping site a defensive and almost isolated position on the plain.

'Do you think,' said Robert to his father, as he saw these arrangements, 'that the Count's lot will *attack* us?'

'No,' said the Major. 'They are fairly certainly less numerous than we, and besides, I think there is a limit of lawlessness beyond which the Count will not go. He wants to delay and dissuade us, not murder us.'

'What's all this for, then?' asked Robert.

'Just in case,' said the Major. 'And for lions,' he added.

Chapter 6

AN ENCOUNTER

I

THE soft purples and browns of the distant eastern hills changed to grey. The greyness, against a sky which also was being drained of colour, seemed suddenly very near. A solitary star began winking above it. In the west the flame-coloured streamers of the sunset stretched across pale green. The five Europeans sat in camp chairs on the spur, sipping their coffee and watching the swift change of day into night. Not far from them, William Kapaki was trimming Joseph's woolly hair with a razor blade and making a horrible scraping sound. Mgambe, wrapped already in his blanket, squatted near the fire watching the *posho* pot, the last light gleaming on his polished brown skull and sparse white hair.

'How far now to the Wazambas?' asked Robert.

Major Brown pointed to the east. 'They are there, among those hills. It doesn't look far, does it? Nor is it, really. About as far as Dover is from London: but we shall be fortunate if we are there by tomorrow night.'

'And how soon shall we see the king, and Dr Maine get permission for his company to mine the gold?'

The Major laughed. 'I wish I knew. The king is not an easy person to deal with.'

'What is he like?' asked Charles. 'Is he very old?'

'No, he is young – not more than twenty-five. Rather

52

plump, rather handsome. His name is Sete. He has been king barely three years. The old king, his father, had two sons by his chief or designated wife – only the sons of the chief wife rank for succession to the throne – Sete and his brother, Lugu. In the last years of the old king's reign there were bitter quarrels between Sete and Lugu about the succession. Lugu maintained that Sete was not a son of the king's by the chief wife – or at all – but had, in infancy, been smuggled into the palace enclosure and substituted for the chief wife's baby which happened to be a girl. This is the usual sort of story which is concocted by the younger brothers of heirs apparent, and I, personally, do not believe it. But Lugu seems to be an intelligent and forceful young man, and he gained a good deal of support in some quarters. On the old king's death Sete tried to have Lugu murdered so as to rid himself permanently of opposition. However, Lugu escaped, and now lives in a remote part of Sete's kingdom with some of his supporters who escaped with him. There has never been any trouble. If there had, I suppose the British Government would have intervened and put it down, and probably placed the Wazamba country under control. But it is all very peaceful, and life goes on there much as it went on when the Wazambas were discovered by white men towards the end of the nineteenth century.'

'Have you seen Lugu?' asked Robert.

'No,' said his father. 'I am glad not to have. Sete's confidence was hard enough to win, and I'm sure that if I ever met Lugu he would be madly suspicious.'

'It sounds very grand with kings and palaces,' remarked Robert.

The Major laughed. 'A rather faded grandeur. A legacy from the old days when the Wazamba was a warlike tribe and sold its prisoners of war to the slave traders. Nowadays they merely keep cattle, and while everyone is pretty comfortably off by African standards, there is not enough wealth for any of the elaborate trimmings of life. And few have bothered since the days of slavery to trade with them, so they value very highly such things as cloth and beads – to say nothing of fire-arms. But the old ritual – the festivals, the ceremony, the dances, the taboos – goes on: a little shabby by now; a provincial touring company instead of the West End production.'

'What about the language, Major Brown?' asked Charles. 'Can they understand Swahili?'

'No. When I first visited them I took an interpreter – a boy who had been to Mission School in Moru; but now I know the language sufficiently well for my own and Dr Maine's purposes.'

It was almost completely dark, and Dr Maine had been compelled to light one of the oil-lamps in order to see to read: it had collected round it already a grotesque collection of insects. The natives had cleared away the meal and were smoking their pipes round the fire. Many stars were glittering in the high sky. Robert strolled to the edge of the spur, and looked out into the darkness.

Suddenly he became aware that what he had unconsciously regarded as the silence of the night was not a silence at all, and that the cool air was filled with a hundred tiny noises. From the herds of animals on the plain came a continual soft padding of hooves, and an occasional cry – a vast uneasy shuffling that filled him, as he listened, with a strange emotion of pity. And then, in the distance, but sharp and reverberating, there snapped out a short roar.

'What was that?' he said to his father, who had walked up behind him. 'A lion?'

'Yes,' said the Major. 'Listen, there it is again.'

Robert shuddered.

'Do you feel that it is terrible?' asked the Major. 'I always do. I think it is the knowledge that any one of these animals – which in the daytime seem so noble and free, and at night so humanly fated and helpless – may be selected by the lion and killed in the darkness.'

Robert considered. 'Yes, it's like some story where a town has to offer up some innocent victim every day to appease a dragon.'

'These sort of scenes,' said Major Brown, 'in the past life of now civilized races, no doubt provided the inspiration for those sort of stories. When we see what we are seeing now, life seems to be governed by nothing except cruelty and chance. To make life acceptable we should have to invent a lion legend, and give both the killer and the victim more satisfactory motives – in fact, relate them to a system of morality.'

He lit a cigarette. 'However,' he went on, 'perhaps it is all no more shocking than Dr Maine's and Curnow's respective gold companies. But don't tell Maine I said so.'

II

In the tents, on the camp beds, muffled in mosquito nets, everyone (except Mr Craig, who was still troubled with the digestion of corned beef) slept very well. They were up early in the keen morning air to a breakfast of tinned plums, cheese and oatcakes, and coffee. No doubt the Count and Mr Yang were somewhere breakfasting off the tinned grapefruit and bacon which Major Brown had originally ordered. After breakfast the cars were loaded up and began to move off.

They had all to manoeuvre to come down the spur, and then to break through the thick bushes which fringed the river bed. Mr Craig and Joseph in the Dodge happened to be first. As their car entered the bushes a huge lioness ran in front of them and vanished in the long grass on the opposite side of the river.

Mr Craig, stimulated, perhaps, by his cheese breakfast, stood up in the car and called to Major Brown. 'Brown, I intend to get *something* out of this trip – I shall shoot that lion. I have lived fifteen years in this country, and never been so near to one before.'

Major Brown looked extremely dubious. But Dr Maine was already out of the Ford, and, walking up to the Major, said: 'I think we owe it to him.'

'Well,' said the Major, gloomily, 'I hope you both realize the risk. But we must start off in half an hour, whether you've got it by then or not. I am dead against this, you know.'

Mr Craig made light of the Major's objections. 'There are

three of us, Brown – don't be so timid. All work and no lion-shooting makes Jack a dull boy.'

At this unusual facetiousness Major Brown became more despondent than ever. But Mgambe was delighted at the break in the routine. He had had the rifles ready all the journey, and now handed them lovingly out. Robert and Charles were ordered, despite their protests, to watch things from the safety of the Ford. Mr Craig, backed up by Dr Maine and the Major, descended to the parched channel of the river. Joseph, with his new haircut and squinting horribly, apparently regarded lion-hunting as all in the day's work of a chauffeur, and with William, under Mgambe's direction, began to beat the grass in which Mr Craig hoped, and the Major did not hope, the lion was hiding.

Robert, half apprehensive, half excited, and with a wholly alive stomach, had his eyes glued on the thick, flaxen undergrowth. From time to time it was stirred by the breeze, and at those moments Robert's heart shot into his mouth.

Four slow minutes passed. Robert's feelings began to change: the lion, he thought, would not come out; it had run right through the grass, and was at this moment loping over the plain half a mile away. Mr Craig was evidently of the same mind: he took a few seconds off to push back the wide-brimmed felt hat which rather swamped his tiny head, and to wipe his sweaty face with a handkerchief.

At that moment the head of the lioness appeared not twenty yards from him, framed in the grass as though it were a stuffed head mounted on a wall. He dropped the handkerchief and fumbled with his rifle. The lioness came out of the grass at a run. Yellow, with a suède-like dullness and smoothness about its coat, it moved with a powerful, shambling grace. Mr Craig hurriedly raised his rifle, and, firing from fifteen yards and aiming at the beast's heart, carefully missed it altogether.

The detonation and the *whee* of the bullet sent a fresh pulse throbbing in Robert's belly. With horror, he saw the animal stop dead and draw back on her haunches, her body close to the ground. Then Dr Maine and Major Brown fired together.

Both bullets hit the lioness, and her spring carried her only a feeble few feet. She slithered over the dried mud, and then lay unmoving. Robert and Charles uttered, from the van, cries of triumph.

Dr Maine ran up to the beast. The Major and Mgambe cried out to him to keep back, but they were too late. When Dr Maine was almost on her she rose, as from the dead, to her round, menacing feet, and made ready to spring again. Dr Maine had no time to raise his rifle. Desperately, he fell flat on his face.

But at this point Mr Craig came into the picture again. By now he had prepared himself for his second shot, and his preparations being of a slightly ponderous nature they had gone on despite the hits by the other two. Mr Craig fired again, and this time made no mistake. The head of the lioness dropped, and she twitched over on to her side.

'Good shot, Craig,' said Dr Maine, with astonishing calm, getting to his feet and brushing down his black alpaca jacket.

'The same to you,' said Mr Craig, extremely pleased with himself.

Major Brown spoke in the righteous and knowing tones of one who had been against the escapade from the start. 'What on earth happened to your first shot, Craig? What possessed you to run up to the animal like that, Maine? It's a miracle that you were not clawed to death – both of you.'

'Three of us,' said Mr Craig. 'I said three of us would be enough.'

Robert and Charles scrambled out of the Ford, and came excitedly to inspect the kill. Their movement coincided with the appearance of a second lion, which strolled leisurely out of the tall grass.

III

It was a male, with a magnificent black mane, and a calm masterful turned-down mouth. Its tail threshed. All were petrified. Robert and Charles were between the lion and the three white men, in the line of fire. Not that Dr Maine could have fired; his rifle still lay on the ground where he had dropped it when the lioness had come to life. Mr Craig was also unarmed: after his successful second shot he had handed his rifle to Mgambe. Major Brown's rifle was instantly at his shoulder, but his view of the lion was impeded by his son's head. A sweat broke out over the whole of his body.

'Get down,' he hissed to the two boys.

The lion started to advance towards the body of the lioness. It was uneasy and nervous.

'Get down,' croaked the Major again.

The boys still stood like a pair of statues.

But in the few seconds which had elapsed since the lion's appearance, Mgambe, with Mr Craig's rifle, had moved a few silent paces, and calmly, after making sure with a glance that none of the white men were able to fire, shot the lion through the head.

The explosion brought the boys to life: they dropped to the ground, and Major Brown immediately fired a second shot into the lion over their recumbent bodies.

William and Joseph jumped into the air with wild cries of excitement. Mgambe ran to Major Brown, apologizing for taking the shot.

'My dear Mgambe,' said the Major, with emotion, 'you must not say you are sorry. I owe you a debt which I shall never be able to repay. I foresaw my son's death, which you averted.'

He took the old man by the hand, and shook it warmly. Mgambe's wrinkled face was solemn, as befitted the serious occasion, but his eyes were filled with pleasure.

Mr Craig at last found time to straighten his hat. '*Two* lions,' he said, with awe. 'Perhaps you were right after all, Brown.'

Robert and Charles were tittering a little hysterically. The Major still held Mgambe's hand, and was now speechless.

Only Dr Maine seemed to have something calm and concrete to say. 'Fetch a bottle of brandy from the car,' he called firmly to William.

IV

The three natives skinned the lions rapidly, Mgambe removing the masks from the skulls with a beautiful deftness. The once-noble beasts were reduced to the status of goods in a butcher's shop; a transformation which Robert could not bear to look at. The pelts were carefully scraped, and pegged to the roof of the Ford to dry in the sun. Much delayed, the cars again started off. Looking back to the spur, as they lurched along the river bed, Robert saw the vultures already spiralling down the clear air to the carcasses. From the car in which Mgambe sat came coils of blue smoke, the wreaths of a new and fat plug of tobacco bequeathed to him by Major Brown.

By three o'clock they had crossed the plain and were beneath the hills which, as they approached, had grown gradually taller and more focused and now presented a steep, rocky, wrinkled, greyish-brown face: a grim inaccessibility which dismayed Robert.

'How are we to get up there?' he asked his father.

'We drive round them a little, and then there is a track of sorts which I am hoping will be wide enough for the van. If it isn't Joseph will have to take the wretched thing back to Makala. If we only had those box bodies!'

The track was awful and the gradient frightening. With boiling radiators the cars crawled up. Half-way, one of the sharp flints which littered the track punctured the Dodge's rear off-side tyre, and the car finished the climb grinding horribly on the rim. In spite of a few anxious moments, the track accommodated the Ford. At the top, while the tyre was being changed, they had tea.

'The last of the water,' said Major Brown. 'It is as well we didn't stay on the plain to shoot any more lions.'

'I suppose I shall never hear the last of those lions,' said Mr Craig.

The country had now changed its character utterly. Before them falling gently away, was a rolling grassland of an intense green, and in the distance the still more vivid green of trees.

Robert and Charles ran to the edge of the heights they had just ascended, and saw before them, like a great map, the entire plain: lion-coloured, with the scrubby thorn trees stippling it lightly with brown. Two giraffes, like twigs, moved across it. It was gashed with the green of the watercourses. In the distance the plain faded into the haze which hung round the horizon.

Not only this magnificent scene, but also, when they moved off after tea, the apparently endless succession of gentle hills and valleys, impressed Robert forcibly with the uncanny size of the country. And although now they began to come across groups of cylindrical thatched huts, there was still the curious feeling that man, in his sparsity and tininess, was far less important than the nature which here took such solemn and gigantic forms.

There were herds of small humped African cattle grazing on the slopes. The inhabitants of the country were visible only as occasional faces peering round the doorways of the huts. The expedition had either caused them alarm or else they were blasé.

'Which?' inquired Robert.

'Blasé,' said his father. 'You must remember that the Wazambas have had a civilization of a kind for many, many years, and they have not altogether lost their pride.'

The grassland gave place to a forest, the edge of which the cars started to pierce on a track so narrow that their mudguards tore the undergrowth on either side. In the semigloom, great butterflies fluttered before them, their wings – lime-green, purple, lemon – catching the powdered shafts of sunlight which sifted through the branches. Once, Robert saw a monkey swinging like a grey acrobat high in the tree tops. The track wound and dipped. It had certainly not been designed to accommodate a motor car. Often, the expedition had to stop and remove tree trunks from the way. But the Major pressed on over the difficulties, eager to be out of the forest before the sun went down.

At last the trees ended. The ground fell away in an immense slope. At the bottom, where a swift and glittering river ran through its fringing trees, an impressive array of huts appeared. The smoke of domestic fires hung like threads in the still evening air. Far in the distance rose a blue line of mountains: on the highest peak lay a breath-taking sheet of snow.

'We are there,' said Major Brown, putting on his brakes, and fumbling for the reward of a cigarette.

Chapter 7

WAITING

I

IN far too short a time for it to have been prompted by the sight of the expedition – in the strange African way the news of its coming must have travelled before it – a procession began to climb the slope from the town. It was made up mainly of small children, but at the head of it were two men, one young, the other old. The young man carried a spear, the old man a long thin stick which helped him as he trotted nimbly along. The children stopped at a respectful distance from the stationary cars, but the two men walked up to the Major. The old man bowed. His face was as wrinkled as a peach stone. An earth-coloured skin covered his shoulders; apart from that and a loincloth, he was naked. He started speaking to the Major. It was a long speech, evidently of a formal nature. At the end of it he relaxed, smiled, and spoke a few more words. Major Brown smiled, too, and held out his hand. The old man shook it. They had a long conversation. Dr Maine, Mr Craig, Robert, and Charles gathered round, trying to tell from the expression of the speakers what it was all about. The Major began to look grave, and to speak sternly.

At length both the old man and the young man turned round and walked back down the hill. After some hesitation the children followed them, and the expedition was left alone.

'What was all that about?' asked Dr Maine.

'Bad news,' said the Major, gazing after the procession.

'Oh dear,' wailed Mr Craig.

'The old man was one of Sete's counsellors: he is called Tetu. He helped me very much when I was here before. The young man was merely one of Sete's warriors. Tetu says that three strange men arrived this morning.'

'Curnow, Yang and the rascally taxi-driver,' exclaimed Dr Maine.

'Yes,' said the Major. 'There is one white man, whom Tetu described as being fatter than the Wazamba women, who are prized for their corpulence. Another man is the colour of butter, and the third is brown like the Wazambas.'

'Has Curnow seen Sete yet?' asked Dr Maine.

'Apparently not. But there is a difficulty more immediate than your blessed gold. Curnow has already sent Sete some handsome presents, and in return Sete has given Curnow the use of the guest huts just outside the palace enclosure, where I lived the last time and where I intended we should all live this time. There is no other accommodation which would suit our dignity.'

'We shall have to live in the tents, then?'

The Major nodded.

Mr Craig's dismay was pathetic. 'Maine, you must settle with Sete about the concession without any delay at all. I simply cannot stand tent life.'

'What I am worried about,' said Dr Maine, 'is that Curnow will see Sete first.'

'I shouldn't be too worried,' said the Major. 'Curnow will not gain Sete's confidence or get a concession merely by giving presents – however handsome. He has won the first round, but it isn't a very important one except that it affects our comfort.'

Mr Craig coughed meaningly. 'I hope I don't appear a mere materialist, but I regard our comfort as highly important. There is also another vital matter; the question of, not to put too fine a point on it, food. Is Sete going to be as generous to us with food as he has been with huts?'

'I have asked Tetu to see that we have food,' said Major Brown. 'Tomorrow we will send Sete a present and ask him to see us. In the meantime, let's try and make ourselves as comfortable as we can.'

A fire was lighted and the tents pitched round it. The three Africans went to the river for water. The sun went down. They all sat by the fire waiting for the food from Sete. Among the luggage unpacked from the cars was a small black case, which, when Dr Maine opened it, proved to contain a flute. Sitting on his camp chair, the orange light glowing on his pale face and dark glasses, he solemnly played some florid tunes by Handel. William, Joseph, and Mgambe, returning with the canvas buckets, were ravished by the music. Even Mr Craig beat his hand, soulfully, but out of time.

But although they delayed supper until after eight o'clock, no food arrived from the palace. In the end, amid Mr Craig's groans, the Major furiously ordered tins of bully beef to be opened.

II

The next morning, Tetu arrived before breakfast: with him was a small boy carrying two hens – Sete's gift of food.

Major Brown was more furious than ever at this piddling present. 'I shall send them back. It is insolence on Sete's part.'

'Please don't,' wailed Mr Craig. 'A wing, and a *tiny* slice of the white meat is all I ask.'

Maine was anxious, too. 'Don't you think we might antagonize Sete by sending the wretched things back? Remember, I'm here as a gold miner not an anthropologist.'

'Curnow's arrival *and* ours have given Sete false ideas of his own importance,' said the Major. 'We must not be intimidated. If we accept these two miserable birds Sete will think he can do what he likes with us.'

Mr Craig bravely turned his eyes from the hens. 'Alas, Brown is absolutely right. If we don't return this lot, the next lot of food will consist of one hen, and the next half a dozen eggs, and so on – until we are starved out. It is high time this country was put under proper control. A hard-headed magistrate and a regiment of *askaris* – that's all that is required.'

'All right,' said Dr Maine. 'Do what you like with the hens. Do you think Sete knows what Curnow and I are after?'

'No,' replied the Major. 'Sete is just being humorous. I shall send back these fowls, and then, in an hour, dispatch William Kapaki to the palace with a gift of one of the lion skins and the clock with the Westminster chimes. Sete must be made to understand that we will not be treated like children.'

The Major then turned to Tetu (who had been standing all this time with an embarrassed expression) and spoke to him seriously. Then Tetu, the small boy, and the two hens, departed the way they had come.

In due course, William left for the palace with the lion skin rolled up and tied to his back, and carrying (as well as his cap with flaps) the large and hideous clock on his head. The chimes rang out incongruously as he walked down the hill.

When he had gone there seemed nothing to do but wait for events to happen. Dr Maine took out his flute again and played, over and over, a sad melody by Gluck: he felt keenly that things were not going well. The Major wrote up his diary, making a secret note in Hindustani that 'in the long run, Craig, astonishingly, may prove more useful and reliable than Maine!' Mr Craig, missing the nine-hole golf course at Moru, filed his finger nails in a bored manner, gazing at a two-month-old copy of *The Times*. Robert and Charles got out the telescope, and, training it on the town, tried to espy the Count or Yang or even the African with the feathers in his helmet.

The huts lay peacefully in the sun: the smoke rose, the clouds were uncoiling from the great mountain peaks in the distance. The agents of the Consolidated Mining Company were not visible to spoil a scene which, for hundreds of years, had scarcely changed.

Robert fretted with impatience: he was anxious not only to

see King Sete, the palace, and the court, but also for Dr Maine's business to be brought to a happy end. It seemed to him that with the Count settled in the guest huts at the palace gates, the whole beautiful country was menaced. Although the Count was sending presents and trying to please Sete, the king and his subjects were already in danger of being disintegrated by the forces which the Count represented. And, as he thought about it more, Robert saw that Dr Maine, too, was a representative – although one of good will – of the same forces. The world which had produced Dr Maine's hat, and even his father's science, could not live side by side with Sete's world. Though he did not quite see how, he knew that these expeditions must change the Wazambas, permanently and deeply.

III

William Kapaki did not return from the palace until early afternoon: he had been kept waiting in the forecourt for hours before Sete had sent a member of his entourage to receive the presents. Tetu did not visit them again until early evening: he brought a message that the king would see them in the morning of the following day. Tetu was accompanied by young men bearing a calf, three hens, two large vessels full of milk and another of the Wazamba beer, a stalk of bananas and a basket of sweet potatoes.

'Salvation for my stomach!' cried Mr Craig, when he saw all this.

'What did the trick?' asked Maine. 'The lion skin or the clock?'

The Major was more dubious about Sete's change of attitude. He questioned Tetu, who said that Sete had also arranged to see Count Curnow the next day – in the afternoon.

'I shall not be happy,' said the Major, dipping a finger in the beer and licking it with a shudder, 'until we have completed negotiations with Sete, and seen Curnow leave. If ever that happy day comes.'

'I think we have gained a victory,' said Dr Maine, 'in that

Sete is seeing us first. Or, rather, you have gained a victory, Brown.'

The Major said: 'I shall tell Sete immediately what you are here for, Maine. I shan't give him details, but I shall whet his curiosity. I shall also warn him against Curnow.'

'Lay it on thick,' said Dr Maine. 'And do you think we ought to send him the other lion skin?'

The heart-warming smell of roast veal began to drift over from the fire.

Chapter 8

MORE WAITING

I

THE next day Mgambe and Joseph were left to guard the camp while the rest of the party set out to visit Sete. William Kapaki wore his brogues and carried his ostrich-headed walking stick: everyone, indeed, had some mark of splendour – even Mr Craig had changed his spectacles for an impressive pair of pince-nez with a thick black ribbon. Robert thought that Charles might also have changed, with advantage, *his* spectacles.

The town could only by courtesy be called a town. There were no stone buildings: the mud-brick and thatched huts were so arranged as to make a main street, but the street was only trodden earth. At the end of it, on rising ground by the river, was a bamboo palisade, a man's height. Towards this they walked.

Just outside the palisade was a group of huts larger than the rest.

'The guest huts,' said the Major to Robert, who was walking at his side. 'Look out for your friend.'

Robert blushed, but cautiously turned his head as they drew near, partly curious, partly embarrassed, and partly –

though he was, he knew, not in the least danger – with a vague fear. There, in a deck chair on the veranda of one of the huts, was Count Hugo Curnow. On his white suit was a splash of purple which Robert recognized as the lizard, Nietzsche. A purple handkerchief to match covered the Count's face and head. Robert hoped he was asleep.

But as the procession drew level with him, the Count suddenly snatched the handkerchief from his hairless dome, opened his eyes, saw Robert, and smiled. Robert, quite disgracefully, felt immediately ashamed of his companions: of Mr Craig's absurd (it seemed to him then) pince-nez, of Charles' unmended spectacles and unbrushed hair, of William Kapaki's grinning innocence.

'Good morning, dear boy,' called the Count. 'We meet again.'

'Good morning,' replied Robert, faintly.

'Will you introduce me to Curnow?' whispered Major Brown.

'Introduce you!' exclaimed Robert. 'Oh, Father!'

'I'm serious.'

Major Brown and Robert walked over to the hut. The Count, still smiling, rose to his feet.

'This is truly delightful, Robert,' he murmured.

'Count Curnow, this is my father, Major Brown. Richard, this is Count Hugo Curnow,' said Robert, in a voice which trembled at the edges.

The Count gracefully put Nietzsche in his pocket with one hand, and held out the other. Major Brown looked at the hand, and said: 'I did not come over to you to shake hands.'

The Count let his hand fall, smiling still and not turning a hair. The Major's weather-beaten face was very serious, his stocky figure upright in his best Army manner.

'I know that in the world of big business,' he went on, becoming, in his embarrassment, a bit pompous, 'a world in which I have now concerned myself, violence behind the scenes is not uncommon. But I'm shocked to find children involved in the violence. I warn you that any future action against Robert by you or your employees will entail serious consequences for you.' The Major coughed loudly. 'Very serious.'

'Major Brown,' said the Count, in expressive tones, 'I am truly sorry for what happened in Mombasa.'

'And Makala,' Robert could not help saying.

The Count tittered. 'Nothing happened in Makala – alas! As I say, I am sorry. Unfortunately, my company practically *forces* me to use the most unscrupulous methods on its behalf. However, it looks as though Robert will be put to no more inconvenience. I see His Majesty this afternoon. You are on your way to see him now, I presume?'

Major Brown did not answer, but made a military about-turn, and went off with Robert to join the others.

'Robert,' said Charles, 'you looked terrified.'

Robert coloured. 'I *was* terrified.'

'Even with papa there?'

The Major was talking to the other men. 'I was terrified *for* my father,' whispered Robert. 'My extreme youth protects me, but I'm sure the Count would have as soon shot Richard as said how-d'you-do.'

'Hem,' said Charles.

The procession moved on. It was met, at the gate in the palisade, by Tetu, who led the way to a large hut without sides, spread with mats.

'The waiting-room,' explained the Major, sitting down on the mats. 'Make yourselves as comfortable as you can. If Sete is in a silly, regal mood, we shall be here some time.'

Inside the palisade was what seemed another village. A variety of huts were set out in a haphazard manner; children played on the dry earth, old men squatted in the shade, bulky female forms could be seen through the open doorways. Sacred cows, theoretically white but in reality red with dust, wandered at large, eating the thatch of the huts, the grass mats in the waiting-room, and making everywhere insanitary. It became very hot: flies pinged down from the roof on to the necks of the expedition, biting like mad dogs. After an hour everyone was sticky, itchy, and bored.

At last the hard-worked Tetu appeared again, and spoke to

Major Brown. When he had finished the Major said: 'Sete's aunt wants to see us.'

'Sete's aunt!' exclaimed Dr Maine.

'She has influence with the king,' said the Major, soothingly. 'I don't think it would be a bad idea to see her while we are waiting for Sete.'

'Really –' Dr Maine considerately swallowed his protest.

'In my opinion,' grumbled Mr Craig, 'we should do as much good by seeing Charley's aunt.'

'Ha, ha!' said Dr Maine, unamusedly.

Tetu led the way to a large hut through which, among giggling and gigantic women, they all passed, coming out on a spacious veranda, shaded not only by its thatch but by trees which grew within a few feet. At the end of it, reclining on flat cushions, with one girl to fan her and another with a switch to beat off the flies, was Sete's aunt. A young boy sat at her feet, replenishing her drinking cup at frequent intervals from a large basin.

II

Sete's aunt greeted the Major with a wide smile and a flow of talk. He bowed solemnly, and, advancing towards her, gallantly took her hand and raised it to his lips. She was delighted, and nudged her handmaidens so as to make sure that they were observing what was going on. Major Brown then introduced his party one by one: Robert wondering apprehensively whether he, too, would have to kiss the lady's hand. But Dr Maine set the precedent by making, as his name was mentioned, a profound bow. Sete's aunt was still more delighted as each member of the expedition stood before her, commenting and gesturing to her attendants with the utmost frankness on his salient characteristics. At Dr Maine's hat, as he removed it and bowed, she pointed with a shriek of laughter: she peered gravely at Mr Craig's pince-nez: Charles Craig's straight and lemon-coloured hair excited all her wonder – indeed, as he bowed, she reached up and tried to stroke it, thereby shaking somewhat his attitude of scientific detachment.

When all this was over and she had composed herself with a draught from her drinking cup, she told the Major that they might be seated on the cushions which had been brought for them. Then (as he related afterwards) she questioned the Major on the reasons for his return to the Wazambas with such a large and interesting party. He thought it advisable not to conceal the truth from her, and told her that wealthy and powerful white men, whom Dr Maine represented, wished to enter the country and engage in vast works which would make the Wazambas wealthy beyond anything they had dreamed. She was not particularly impressed. The Wazambas, she pointed out, were already wealthy. She had seen many visiting white men who had in one way or another, promised riches; but the Wazambas disliked trade and loved independence. What she was really interested in were *people*. Dr Maine, now; what function did he perform among the white men which gave him the right to wear such astonishing clothes? How many wives, how many children had he?

Major Brown did not press her to talk about the project of the African Gold Company. He had planted the seed of the idea in her head, and was satisfied. Her blasé attitude towards it he did not entirely believe in: it was probably a kind of bluff, the automatic bluff of the African as a defence against the likelihood of being done down.

Suddenly, Sete's aunt asked what the other expedition was, the expedition which her nephew had lodged importantly in the guest huts. Major Brown said that it was an expedition to swindle the Wazambas.

Sete's aunt hooted with laughter, a paroxysm of disbelief, and rolled about on her cushions. She ended on her stomach, her face buried.

Mr Craig, with surprising facetiousness and vulgarity, said: 'The biggest bottom in Africa.'

Sete's aunt was certainly a massive woman, even among the Wazambas, whose women drink excessive quantities of milk so as to put on the desirable weight, and where the absolute of female beauty is immovability. Her head was shaven and oiled so that it appeared to be made of caramel. Bluish tattooing lined her shaking cheeks. About five pounds of copper wire were wound round her neck: a somewhat less amount was coiled through holes in the distorted lobes of her ears. She wore a kind of toga, of neutral-coloured native cloth, on which were sewn thousands of tiny beads in a regular and repetitive design. She was in her middle forties – already, by the standards of her race, an old woman.

At last she peeped out of her cushions in mock shyness. With a frightening show of coquetry she fixed her eye on Dr Maine and beckoned him to sit down beside her.

'Not for all the gold in Africa!' said Dr Maine, backing away.

'Come, Maine,' said the Major, keeping his face wonderfully straight. 'She is very influential. You must not offend her.'

'No, *no*!' cried Maine. 'Make some excuse. Say I've got leprosy.'

'Very well,' said Major Brown, 'but I think you are throwing your company's chances away.'

Dr Maine shuddered. The Major then told Sete's aunt that Dr Maine's chief wife was abnormally, ferociously jealous, and that he therefore dare not go near another woman, especially one so exalted and attractive. Sete's aunt was enthralled but dubious. Where was Dr Maine's jealous wife? In the white man's country, the Major replied. Then how could she know if Dr Maine misbehaved himself a little. Because she was a powerful witch, said Major Brown, solemnly. This completely satisfied Sete's aunt. She took a draught from her drinking cup, and hiccuped resoundingly.

'The woman's as tight as an owl,' said Mr Craig.

III

Sete's aunt at length dismissed the expedition, and withdrew into her hut to sleep. No message had come from Sete, and since it was then long past lunch-time the Major thought it prudent, as well as dignified, to return to camp without further waiting. Sete's aunt, the heat, the sense of frustration, had exhausted everyone. Tetu did not appear, so they marched out of the palace enclosure and through the village without a word to anyone, leaving Sete to draw his own conclusions. The veranda of the Count's hut was empty: doubtless after an early and ample lunch he was taking a siesta to prepare himself for negotiations with Sete. The party passed sourly and hungrily.

Towards evening a flustered Tetu came to the camp. Why, he said, had the expedition left the palace so hurriedly? The king was disappointed and hurt. Rubbish, said Major Brown. Tetu became still more flustered. Would the party visit the king the next day? Yes, said Major Brown – but only if Sete gave it an audience promptly. Tetu said that would certainly happen. Today, the king had not been well, and also had had much official business. He had heard disquieting reports about his ambitious brother, Lugu. Tetu started on a rambling story. The Major interrupted him: had Sete seen the other white man today? After some talking round the subject Tetu admitted that the king had interviewed Count Curnow. But, added Tetu hastily, the king was much displeased with him. No one could take the place of Major Brown in Sete's heart.

All this was related by the Major when Tetu had gone.

'Curnow has beaten us again,' commented the Major, gloomily, 'and I can't understand why.'

'I thought you were influential in this country,' remarked Mr Craig, with mild sarcasm.

'The king being displeased with Curnow is an invention of Tetu's, I suppose,' said Dr Maine.

'Almost certainly,' said the Major. 'The African loves to make people feel happy even though it means a distortion of the truth.'

'Well, perhaps we shall get somewhere tomorrow,' said Maine.

Mr Craig removed his pince-nez to polish them, and looked ruefully at their smart black ribbon. 'Maine,' he said, 'you should have been more friendly with Sete's aunt.'

Chapter 9

THE KING

I

THAT night Robert and Charles lay for a long time awake in the tent they shared between them. From the inside of his mosquito net Charles sprayed, with a syringe of insecticide, the insects which settled on the outside. After an exhausting effort he succeeded in making a grasshopper-like creature, the size of a fountain-pen, topple off the net to the ground.

'Twenty-eight sprays,' breathed Charles. 'This is a highly inefficient insecticide.'

'I think you drowned the beast, not poisoned it,' said Robert. 'The stuff's about as efficient as this expedition.'

'Mm,' said Charles. 'It certainly looks as though we shall be here until school starts again. What a bore! I'd planned to catch and dissect an iguana.'

'I don't think my father is forceful enough,' said Robert.

'Mine certainly isn't.'

'The expedition ought to throw its weight about a bit. I'm very disappointed with Dr Maine. I thought he was a man of action. That flute playing is about the last thing.'

'Yes,' said Charles. 'I give him a black mark for the flute.'

'Can *we* do anything?'

'Very difficult. What do you suggest?'

Robert thought. 'If there were an eclipse tomorrow we could threaten Sete that unless he saw the expedition, and granted the concession, we would put out the sun.'

'Unfortunately, there is no eclipse of the sun tomorrow. There is one of the moon next January, but that is not of immediate use. We may still be here then, of course.'

'I suppose,' sighed Robert, 'that we're just as helpless as the rest of them.'

'Just,' said Charles, squirting his syringe at a great moth. 'It's the country that's the trouble. Nothing's been done quickly in Central Africa, ever.'

'Perhaps my father really isn't doing badly at all.'

'I'm sure he's doing well,' said Charles.

'And perhaps you misjudge yours,' said Robert.

'Perhaps.'

'And,' Robert went on relentlessly, 'probably Dr Maine is the very best man for his job.'

'Probably.' The moth fluttered lethargically out of range. 'Except for the flute.'

II

It was still as hot next day in the waiting-room, and the flies just as numerous. The sacred cows scratched their behinds in a profane way on the corner posts, and the usual small pot-bellied children stood round and watched the expedition with liquid brown eyes. Robert had brought his cricket ball: he and Charles and William played catchers, to the delight of the children and the terror of the cows. Dr Maine read his book: a heavy volume by the Danish philosopher, Kierkegaard. Major Brown smoked. Mr Craig fidgeted.

But they had not very long to wait: in less than an hour Tetu appeared, his toothless mouth open in a grin, and beckoned them forward. At the same time they heard, in the distance, the hollow beating of a drum, and a little dissonant phrase played again and again on what sounded like a rubber band stretched over a tin pan.

Tetu took them through an inner palisade, through a large hut, and out into a square formed by other huts. The music grew louder. At the far side of the square was a thatch awning covering a mass of people, plumes of feathers, bright clothes, spears, and skins. The sun glared down on the trodden red earth and was reflected in tiny points of light from the brown flesh of the people squatting in the square. Through these people the expedition picked its way towards the awning. At a convenient and respectful distance away Major Brown stopped and bowed. Robert, at first, found it hard to pick out King Sete from the group under the awning. In the foreground crouched the musicians with the decorated drums, the fiddles made from gourds and strips of cow-hide, and wooden instruments shaped like clarinets which contributed to the din, however, only an occasional squeak. Behind the musicians were some young warriors, their faces glistening with white paint, like clowns, their hair clotted and red with ochre.

Embedded in the tableau, and giving it movement and confusion, were a number of boys waving cow-tail fly-whisks and palm-leaf fans. In the middle was an extraordinary figure, not identifiable as either man or woman, wearing countless strings of beads, bracelets, amulets, animals' teeth, claws and skins, bunches of reeds; smeared with paint, adorned with tattooing; on whose head rested a great metal bowl from which hung heavy chains. Could this be Sete?

A second later Robert saw that he was mistaken: beside the priest or wizard (it could be nothing less) was the only seated person, a young man wearing a shirt and shorts and a leather belt with pockets for ammunition.

From this congregation came an acrid smell, not disgusting, but penetrating and rich.

The seated young man did not appear to acknowledge the Major's bow; he sat still, staring in front of him, as though in a trance. Major Brown did not speak – it would have been useless, anyway, for in the hubbub Sete could scarcely have heard him. As well as the music, considerable noise was made by various groups of people carrying on all sorts of activities quite unconnected with the audience given by the king to

Major Brown and the expedition. Under the awning, little boys were being scolded for not fanning, or fanning too briskly, or for not refilling the pots of liquor, or for falling over. The warriors were talking and gesturing. The priest's ornaments sent out a jangle as he dithered about in a sort of stationary dance. Among the people in the square, women were feeding their babies, old men were snoring; hens scratched and clucked among them. It was all quite unlike what Robert had imagined.

After a long quarter of an hour of this rather pointless encounter, Sete got up. The Wazambas round him fell aside, leaving a gangway to a hut behind the awning down which Sete disappeared. The music stopped. Tetu beckoned the expedition on, and it followed Sete.

Inside the hut Sete was revealed as a more human figure. He was seated again but only accompanied by three of the warriors and a couple of old men. He was a handsome youth, of a light brown colour; his nose straight and clear-cut in profile, with a well-shaped head. Perhaps he was a bit too handsome: there was something unreliable about the large sepia eyes, something vain about the mouth, the plump body rather too well fed. Two tiny parallel raised gashes ornamented each cheek, giving him, in his European shirt and trousers, a touch of barbarity that was disconcerting. When he smiled (as the Major presented the party to him, one by one) he showed teeth that were filed to points.

The Major started talking. Sete became restless, fingering the pouches on his belt. Major Brown frowned, but persevered. Then the king rose, with a smile that was meant to be disarming, and interrupted the Major's explanation with a speech of his own.

The Major turned to Dr Maine. 'He wants us to go hunting with him.'

'Hunting!' exclaimed Dr Maine, whose first reaction was that the word was being used metaphorically. 'Hunting! Have you told him what we're here for?'

'I've tried to. He is in one of his amiable but difficult moods.'

80

Dr Maine groaned. 'Let's go hunting, then.'

Mr Craig was too disgusted to say anything except to ask that William Kapaki might be allowed to accompany him back to camp. The two boys, remembering their conversation of the night before, looked at each other meaningly, but were delighted to go hunting all the same.

III

Only in the evening, when the Major had related much of what the king had said, was Robert able to make for himself a more or less clear picture of the outing with Sete. To begin with, the vision that the word 'hunting' had conjured up, of rhino or leopard or even wild pig, was quickly dissipated when it was seen how the king proposed to set out. The warriors turned up in full force, together with a representative selection of the whisking and fanning boys, to whom were added two youths bearing a portable canopy to protect Sete from the sun. But the trip, as a hunting trip of some sort, was finally ruined when it was seen that Sete's chief wife and her chattering attendants purposed to be present. This involved the bringing of a litter, for although the queen could be scarcely out of her teens she was as plump as a sow; and besides, walking was thought to be below an important woman's dignity.

Sete urged the Major to send for the rifles, but Major Brown refused, on seeing what a picnic was to take place, making the excuse that they were all under repair. Sete's gun-bearer carried, for the use of the king, an ancient musket, hooped with brass, that looked highly dangerous and was eyed nervously by the Major and Dr Maine. But it turned out that there was no ammunition for it.

'What are the white men going to hunt with?' asked Sete.

Major Brown asked Maine to produce his revolver.

Sete could hardly hold back his mirth. 'What is this?' he inquired. 'To *throw* at the quarry?'

The Major explained that it was a kind of small rifle, and deadly. Sete thought this a good joke, and, calling his warriors, explained it carefully until they all giggled. He asked to have the revolver in his hand, and then, sighting carefully a nearby dog, pretended to throw the weapon at it. Then he could control himself no longer, and burst into laughter at his own jest. Immediately, the warriors all threw their spears at the dog, pinning the wretched animal to the ground, and thus proving the superiority of their weapons. They ran to the spears, wiped the blood off them, and rejoined the party.

Robert felt sick, even at the memory of this: it was his first glimpse of the kind of cruelty and indifference which, he supposed he must subconsciously have known, existed among this childish but complicated people.

The hunting party moved off, out of the palisade and up the gentle slope towards the forest. The first creature they saw was a secretary bird, walking in its grave and absurd way along the bank of the river. Dr Maine pointed to it meaningly, and then took out his revolver and patted it. Sete watched with amused interest. Maine went on ahead of the others until he was within effective range of the bird. Then he levelled his revolver, took leisurely aim, and fired.

At the explosion, the queen and her attendants shrieked like mad women. But the warriors, when they saw the bird drop, jumped high in the air with excitement, and rushed away for the corpse, which they brought back with grins and shouts. Sete was stupefied.

'Such a little thing!' he said, with admiration, over and over again.

He asked to be shown how to fire the revolver. Maine slipped the safety catch on and instructed him. Then the whole party wandered round the outskirts of the wood, looking for a suitable target. After a long search they came upon a fat and lazy bird, like a guinea fowl, perching on a low branch of a tree.

Maine and the king, with great stealth, crept on in front of the main party. When they were not more than ten feet from the tree Maine handed Sete the revolver. Sete raised the revolver gingerly and pointed it shakily at the bird. All held their breaths. Sete shut his eyes and pulled the trigger. After the detonation, the bird was still seen seated on the branch. It stayed there a second or two, then launched itself into space in a blasé way, and flapped off.

Sete threw the revolver to the ground in a half-real, half-assumed temper. No one dared to laugh.

The party proceeded in a lackadaisical fashion. The Major began to talk to Sete.

'I am speaking only as your friend,' he said, quietly. 'It doesn't matter to me, except as your friend and the friend of all the Wazambas, whether you favour Dr Maine or Count Curnow. And I must tell you that the day when the white man enters your country permanently to dig for metal cannot be delayed long. It will be in your lifetime, Sete. The decision which will affect your people for many years lies with you. And even if you put off making it, the powers which Maine and Curnow represent will go to the British king, and he will send soldiers to make you decide.'

Sete became very uneasy as the Major said this, and, looking away into the distance, replied: 'Great questions cannot be answered in a short time.'

The Major went unmercifully on: 'I have found Curnow to be cruel and treacherous, not caring in what manner he gets his wishes so long as he gets them. And this is only in the first stage of his dealings with the Wazambas. What will happen if he gets power here? To your people and you? No doubt when you saw him he was flattering and humble, but that is not the real man: it is a mask to deceive you.'

Sete again answered with a tiresome aphorism: 'Men are judged by their actions.'

The Major ignored it. 'I must ask you plainly, Sete – have you made an agreement with Curnow?'

The king walked on for a few minutes in silence. Then he said: 'You are a great hunter, Brown. I liked the lion skin very much. Tomorrow I shall send you a lot of presents.'

There was another silence.

'I am sometimes a sick man,' said Sete.

Major Brown waited patiently until the point of the conversation should be reached. The fanning and whisking boys and the boys bearing the canopy were getting under Sete's feet; he told them to go away. It was very hot, and the hunting party was going slower and slower. Sete stopped, and faced the Major.

'You have never sent me any stimulants,' he said. His large brown eyes were only on the Major's for an instant, and then they slid slyly away.

Everything was then very much clearer to Major Brown. By 'stimulants' Sete meant intoxicating drinks – whisky, gin, rum. Before the Major could answer, Robert let out a shout. A huge hare had jumped from a hole almost beneath his feet, and was bounding down the hill. Dr Maine blazed away at it with his revolver, hit it with a lucky shot, and it went rolling over and over. The women shrieked again; the warriors ran and brought it back, its legs still twitching.

The king professed himself much pleased, declared the hunting trip at an end, shook hands with the Major and Dr Maine, and took himself off with his retinue to the palace.

Tetu, who had stayed behind, came up and said that the king had ordered a dance for the next night, in honour of the white men.

'*All* the white men?' asked the Major.

Tetu looked uneasy. The king, he said, would be very hurt if Major Brown's party did not witness the dance: surely the mere presence of the fat man would not be objectionable? Very well, said the Major, with bad grace.

IV

'You see – Curnow has obviously been sending spirits to Sete,' said the Major that night. 'And I don't mean ghosts.'

'Precisely what advantage does that give Curnow?' asked Maine.

'Not a great one. But it means that so long as Curnow's supply lasts he can see Sete whenever he likes and put a certain amount of pressure on him, too. It accounts for Sete's unusual friendliness towards Curnow and his dithering attitude towards us.'

'Curnow's whisky has made our clock look sick.'

'Well,' said Mr Craig, who was very depressed at this conversation, 'at least he'll have the clock longer than the whisky. But have we to wait here until Sete drinks all Curnow's booze?'

Robert, who was sitting by the camp fire, listening with a feigned air of indifference, gave Charles a nudge. 'Come on,' he whispered, 'I've got an idea.'

The two boys crept away unnoticed.

Chapter 10

THE DANCE

I

'WHAT is it?' asked Charles, when they had reached the privacy of their tent.

'You remember our talk last night?' said Robert. 'I think the time has now come when we can take action.'

'Who are "we"?' Charles asked, suspiciously.

'You and me,' said Robert.

'Mm,' said Charles. 'Are we going to arrange an eclipse?'

'Really, Charles,' said Robert, 'sometimes you are very like your father – if I may say so without offence to either of you.'

Charles grinned. 'Well, spill it. What sort of action?'

Robert came closer, and lowered his voice. 'It's only a little thing, but it's something the adult members of this expedition will never do: (a) because they have too many scruples about law and order, and so on, and (b) because they wouldn't think of it anyway.'

'You interest me strangely,' said Charles.

Robert continued. 'Bottles of spirits have become an important weapon in this battle for Sete's confidence. *We* have no spirits, and shouldn't supply them to Sete even if we had. Therefore the only thing to do is to see that the Count stops supplying them. And the only way to do this – we can't appeal to his better nature or anything – is to destroy the Count's supply.'

'You've got something.'

'It won't be easy, of course,' said Robert. 'But it shouldn't be impossible.'

'The dance!' exclaimed Charles.

'Yes,' said Robert, 'I'd thought of that. We must do it to-morrow night or never. The Count will certainly be watching the dance – and probably Yang and the taxi-driver as well. That gives us an opportunity to get in, at worst, one or other of the guest huts, with a decent chance of finding the spirit, or some of it.'

'It may still be in their cars, of course.'

'All the better if it is. But it's more likely to be in the huts.'

Charles began to work off his excitement with the insect spray. 'I suppose,' he said, 'it's no use mentioning this plan to anyone.'

'Not likely. They'd clamp down on it like hyenas. Neither your papa nor mine would ever approve of anything that wasn't absolutely legal. Dr Maine might be more sympathetic, but he wouldn't go against the others.'

'We play a Lone Hand, then,' said Charles, twirling an imaginary moustache.

'Yes. And as for plans, all we've got to see about, I think, is that we have a hammer or other blunt instrument handy. A spanner from one of the car tool boxes will do. In fact, I'll go and steal it now.'

II

Robert dreamed of the raid on the Count's whisky, and all next day thought of nothing else. Sometimes it seemed to him a ridiculous idea, not only dangerous but bound to fail, and then he felt his and Charles' lack of experience very much. At other times the thing seemed plausible and brilliant. But all the time, knowing how strongly his father and Mr Craig would disapprove, his conscience pricked distressingly.

In the morning, Tetu appeared. At the sight of his amiable and furrowed face Mr Craig groaned: indeed, everyone felt a desire to scream slightly at this embodiment of the expedition's ineffectualness. The old man bowed, and, asking anxiously if a visit was being made to the king, desired to be of assistance.

'This man is a Jonah,' said Mr Craig. 'I have felt so from the beginning. He has no more influence over Sete than I have over my stomach.'

'Is it worth visiting Sete again?' Dr Maine asked the Major.

'Yes,' said Major Brown. 'If Sete is available we ought to peg away at him. You and I will go with Tetu.'

'Come along, boys,' said Mr Craig, decidedly, '*we* will do something useful. We'll go and try to shoot a guinea fowl for lunch.'

When the shooting party returned to camp, rather more than an hour later, they found that Maine and the Major had got back before them.

'Any luck?' said Robert to his father.

Major Brown grimaced. 'Sete was dead drunk. On the Count's whisky, of course.'

'At eleven o'clock in the morning?' Mr Craig shook his head, gloomily. 'It's hopeless. We shall have to ask Government for a company of *askaris* in the end. And that, as you know, will take a year to get. By that time Curnow's company will have dug a mine a mile deep, and King Sete will be in a home for inebriates. But pray look at this wonderful bird. Do you think William can roast it successfully?'

'Didn't you get anything out of Sete at all?' asked Robert.

'Nothing,' said the Major.

Robert clutched the friendly spanner, hidden in his pocket, and looked at Charles with a face, in its very blankness, full of meaning.

III

Before the sun went down, Major Brown had two of the cars driven to a large open space at the rear of the palisade where the dance was to take place, to serve as grand-stands for the party, and for their head-lamps to light the dancers, at least for part of the time.

As soon as the daylight faded, a slow drum began to beat: it sounded like a pulse in the head. When it was completely dark, some flickering lights could be seen in the village. A moon like a great orange began to come up from behind the mountains. Leaving William and Mgambe to guard the camp, the party walked to the dancing place.

The noise of the drum became louder. It looked as though all the town was gathered round the arena. In the middle, heaps of straw burning, sending out an acrid odour and a fitful illumination. Brown skins gleamed. Smoke rolled into the light and vanished in the outer darkness. The party could hardly hear itself speak for the hubbub of voices and the drum. The cars were found and the party climbed in them: Tetu appeared, with a tribe of small boys bearing fruit and jars of drink, keeping the crowd away from the cars and smiling reassuringly.

Kneeling on the rear seat, Robert could see across the open space to where King Sete sat with his wives under a canopy, surrounded by boys holding flaming torches on poles. Robert looked anxiously for the Count. He found him midway between the Major's party and the king, on the side of the arena (Robert noted with satisfaction) furthest from the town. He was seated in the front of one of his box-bodied cars, next to his villainous driver. Where was Yang? He was not in the car with the Count. Robert went dizzy in the attempt to pick out a yellow face from the hundreds of brown ones among the shadows. But it was hardly likely that he would be separated from the Count if he were here at all. Clearly, he was still at the guest huts – and probably standing guard. Robert suffered a pang of apprehension. Yang would have to be faced.

He whispered out of the corner of his mouth to Charles, who was next to him: 'No Yang.'

'So I see,' muttered Charles. 'Hope his leg is still gammy.'

Suddenly, a figure danced into the middle of the arena. He seemed muffled in a cape, and wore a great mask. Major Brown switched on the head-lamps of the car, and the two swathes of light unrolled and transfixed the leaping figure with a dramatic swiftness which drew from the crowd a gasp of wonder and appreciation. The mask was white, of a face powerful and abstract, larger than life, which seemed to belong in reality to the vibrating body, hairy and massive with straw. The figure carried a wand, to the end of which was fastened a skull, also white; the long skull of some buffalo or antelope, which had a strange alive and human look. The skull was waved over each corner of the crowd in turn.

Robert became aware that the tones of other drums now combined with the first drum which had given warning of the dance, and that the silences between its throbbings were filled with a twitching secondary rhythm. And then over the drums a man's high voice gave out a long phrase, half sung, half spoken, and as the reply came back, softly but full-throatedly, from the crowd, two files of young men and girls rushed into the space with demoniac energy.

With the problem of escaping from the dance, of breaking into the guest huts, of avoiding Yang, in the forefront of his mind, his senses excited by the dancing and music, Robert could hardly keep from crying aloud. He gripped the handle of the car door tightly, and looked at commonplace, familiar things – Charles' much-mended glasses, Dr Maine's hat in the next car – to check his emotion.

The stamping dancers had now raised huge pillars of dust which swam redly through the shafts of light from the cars. The young men and girls formed a double circle into which burst a troop of crouching dancers masked as animals – looking more real than the animals themselves would have done. The priest whom Robert had observed on the first visit to the king now appeared, advancing slowly towards the animals, bedecked even more grotesquely than before, and holding a wand. The animals surrounded him. He began whipping them.

Major Brown, conserving his batteries, switched out the head-lamps of the car: Dr Maine followed suit. More straw was thrown on the smouldering piles, and the shadows flickered again. As the drama of the dance unfolded, the crowd pressed closer, swarming round the cars in spite of Tetu's efforts to keep it off.

Charles gave Robert a nudge. Robert nodded. He leaned over and spoke to his father.

'May we go and sit on the front bumpers? We can't see very well.'

'All right,' said the Major, who was very contentedly smoking a cigar, and making notes in the light from the dashboard. 'But don't get pulled away by the crowd.'

They climbed down from the car. Charles whispered into Robert's ear: 'Easy as pie.'

'So far,' said Robert.

They went to the front of the car, away from the line of vision of Dr Maine, Mr Craig, and Joseph in the other. The space in front of them was clear, but edging up behind the car was the crowd, more excited every minute. As they squatted there, the noises and smells smiting their noses and ears, watching the strangely moving patterns and energies of the dancers, a memory came to Robert of sitting at school in England and his headmaster saying, exasperated with the form's stupidity over the relations of angles made by a line cutting two other and parallel lines: 'If I were an African, I'd do a war-dance.' He said to Charles:

'Life is a very curious thing.'

Charles coughed disapprovingly. 'Have you got the spanner? And the torch?'

'Yes. Let's start edging away.'

They edged away. With only a little movement they found that several brown bodies were between themselves and the car. They stayed within earshot of the Major for some minutes, in case their sneaking away had been noticed, but when no call came after them they bent their bodies double and pushed their way through the crowd. They emerged about fifty feet from the cars, at the side of the palace palisade. The moon was now high in the sky, and the bamboo fence threw a deep shadow into which they ran. The drums of the dance were beating quicker: Robert's heart kept in time.

'I've been thinking about Mr Yang,' said Charles. 'He has a knife, and probably a revolver as well. When he hears us setting to work on the whisky we shall have no chance at all. We've got to out-manoeuvre him. I thought of something like this. I go to the front of the huts, making some but not too much noise, and Yang is attracted to me. In the meantime you have gone round the back, discovered the store-room, and you start bashing about. Yang, on hearing this, rushes to you. I try to delay him as much as possible and yell out when I can't delay him any more, so that you can get away. A very sketchy plan, I know, but I don't see how we can do anything better.'

'Supposing he shoots at you?' asked Robert, anxiously. 'Now we've actually started, it does seem a wild and dangerous affair.'

'He won't shoot unless he's forced to. Too noisy. And I shan't resist, or anything. But you won't have much time.'

'Come on, then,' said Robert. 'Let's get it over.'

They ran along the palisade. It came to an end, and before them, across a small open space, the three guest huts lay silver in the moonlight. It was on the veranda of the middle one that the Count had been reclining: the one nearest to the palace had had an unoccupied look. At the back of the farthest the Count's cars were normally parked.

They had decided to go for the middle one first: mainly because it seemed likely that the Count occupied it alone and Yang would not be in it, but also because the Count would probably have the more valuable stores under his eye – especially the whisky.

'I'm off,' whispered Charles. 'Give me a few seconds.' As he ran lightly towards the huts, Robert felt a glow of affection for him – for his untidy hair, platinum in the moonlight, for the flannel trousers he was growing out of and which reached only to his shins, for his great reliability. Robert solemnly crossed fingers for him.

Before Charles had quite disappeared, Robert himself set off, making a slight detour to avoid notice, aiming at the back of the middle hut. Behind them all was a small plantation of maize. Robert plunged straight into the tall tasselled stalks, and immediately felt confident and protected. The run across the open had not been good in spite of the desertion and the stillness.

He wriggled through the maize and saw before him the three huts. In the far one was the yellow light of a lamp: the middle hut was dark. Robert chuckled nervously to himself with excitement. Nothing could be better: it was five pounds to a pinch of (as he, vulgarly, put it to himself) dog-dirt that Yang was in the far hut. They had forgotten that a light would tell them Yang's whereabouts. Robert prayed that Charles would twig the situation, and refrain from making any noise until Yang actually appeared. He strained his ears: there was the faint throbbing and shouting of the dance, a croaking of frogs from the river, but no other sound. He crept forward.

He had a strange, dream-like feeling that he had done all this before. He remembered suddenly that, indeed, he had – in Makala, when they had followed Yang in the rickshaw, and he had crept through the bushes surrounding the house – Indian Joe's house, as they had afterwards discovered – in which the Count was living. What a fantastic affair he was in!

There was no doorway at the back of the hut. Two small windows – without, of course, glass – gaped darkly in the mud wall. They were at the height of Robert's shoulders. He took a little run at one of them, and by grazing his wrists, almost breaking his breast bone, scrambled through. He stood with his back to the window, gripping the spanner and torch, holding his breath. It was as black as Dr Maine's suit.

And then he was certain that someone was in the room with him. There was a tiny scrabbling noise, as of boots on the hard floor shifting cautiously for a pounce. Thoroughly frightened, as though it were a ghost, he pushed the button of the torch, and painted the room wildly with the beam of light.

A camp bed, a camp chair, a pair of shoes, a canvas bucket, a crumpled white shirt, were illuminated in turn. There was no human figure. But the torchlight fell at last in a corner on a small crawling iridescent creature at which Robert giggled with relief. It was Carlyle, the Count's chameleon.

This, then, was the Count's bedroom. Robert began to search carefully with the torch. It was odd, and somewhat unnerving to come in this way across the Count's personal possessions; Robert felt that to touch them would in some magic way tell the Count of his presence, and in spite of the rational part of his mind he kept flicking the beam of the torch towards the doorway which led to the front room, in order to confirm that the great corpulent figure was not standing, amiable and dangerous, framed in it. The lizards were asleep in their box. On a small packing-case of cigarettes by the bed were two books: *Debits and Credits* and Kafka's *Amerika*. A silver drinking cup by the oil-lamp contained a mixture of gin and drowned moths. A drum of turkish delight was half open and half eaten. Robert resisted a foolish desire to pop a piece into his mouth. Between the bed and the wall were several wooden cases. Three of them were reinforced with metal bands and padlocked, but were too shallow for bottles unless the bottles were laid flat in one row, which in Robert's experience was unlikely. Through the cracks in another case he could see the bright metal and labels of cans. He lugged this carefully on the floor to get at the case underneath – a squarish, plausible case.

What magnificent luck! Stencilled on the wood was a name which even to Robert meant nothing but Scotch whisky. And then he realized that it would have to be opened. How lacking in the most elementary intelligence they had been when they had planned this raid: a spanner to bust the bottles, but not even a penknife to force the case. Robert looked round the room with the half-hopeful, half-despairing helplessness of a man who has cut himself while shaving.

What was Charles doing all this time? Robert's toes began to twitch, his stomach had an urgent emptiness. He had too much to do, too much to think about. He flashed the torch at the windows recklessly, certain that Yang's yellow face was watching him like a cruel but playful cat. No one was there. But he felt he simply had to go and look for Charles, for reassurance that things were not on the point of crashing about his ears. He switched off his torch, and tiptoed into the front room.

There was a wide opening into the veranda and the moonlight and the noise of the drums. The trees were glossy and dark against the navy sky. There was no sign of Charles. Robert sighed and went reluctantly back to the bedroom.

He found, after more feverish investigation, another case of whisky. He seemed to have been in the hut for hours. But he was compelled to search still further for some instrument which would break open the cases. His hand clutching the torch became wet with sweat; his mouth was almost unbearably dry.

And then, in a tin trunk full of the Count's clothes, he found a stout knife in a sheath. More luck! He started prising open one of the cases.

When he raised the lid it groaned against the nails in a tone which seemed to Robert might well reach the ears of Count Curnow sitting in his car at the dance. He stopped and listened a moment and then gritted his teeth and persevered. The dozen bottles lay revealed in their shaped papier-mâché containers. He took them out and, resting them on the floor one by one, knocked off their necks with the spanner. The liquid gurgled out.

A reek of whisky, the essence of a thousand public-houses, filled the hut. Robert wondered whether Yang would smell it from next door. He started on the other case.

He had three bottles left to guillotine and his spanner raised when he heard the shout.

'Mr Yang, Mr Yang, Mr Yang!' floated in from the distance. It was not hard to recognize Charles' voice, hovering uncertainly between soprano and baritone. Robert shoved the torch in his pocket and, with a bottle in one hand and the spanner still in the other, trod lightly into the front room and over to the wide doorway. Pressed against the side of it, he peered out into the veranda. It was quite empty. He sidled along in the shadows until he stood at the extreme edge of the veranda, concealed partially by the low wall of reeds which ran along it.

'Mr Yang, Mr Ya-ang!' The call came again, emerging ambiguously, facetiously, and (to Yang, no doubt) irritatingly from the trees.

But although Robert craned his neck at the next hut and strained his eyes into the darkness beneath the trees, Yang was nowhere visible. Neither, of course, was Charles.

And then, with a shock which brought a hot, horrible, throbbing something from his stomach to his throat, he saw, not three feet from him, on a level with the veranda wall, a head of smooth hair, shining blue-black under the moon. The head was turning slowly to the left and to the right, obviously looking for the source of the voice which had so provocatively been calling its owner's name. The hut stood on high foundations, Yang was small; these things accounted for the curious proximity of Yang's head. Curious and – Robert realized with a start – convenient.

Almost without thinking, he lifted his right hand high in the air. As the spanner reached its zenith his training, his feelings, his whole soul, gathered themselves together and for a second protested at the brutality he was about to commit. How could he hit with iron that shining, human, vulnerable head? And then the spanner fell, followed by the bottle. The head disappeared.

Robert rushed back to the Count's bedroom, and dealt with the two remaining bottles. Charles came panting in.

'Wonderful work,' he said.

'Same to you,' said Robert. 'Did you look at poor Yang? I hope I haven't killed him. First his leg and now his head.'

'You've not killed him. He was born to be hanged. What a stench!'

'You were very clever,' said Robert, 'not to make any noise until the end.'

'I saw the light, of course. So I did nothing until Yang came out of the end hut, and started nosing about. He was making for the middle one when I called out. It sounded so silly shouting "Mr Yang".'

'But very effective.'

'It just shows that plans are all nonsense.'

'Let's get out of here very quickly,' said Robert.

As they passed by the veranda, the Chinese was stirring a little: he even stared at them, but with glazed, unseeing eyes. They galloped along the palisade. The drums and the cries grew louder.

The dance was becoming saturnalian, and they could hardly filter themselves through the mass of stamping people to the cars.

'Where on earth have you been?' demanded Major Brown. He had to shout to make himself heard.

'We got carried away,' replied Robert.

'Eh?'

'Carried away,' Robert repeated.

'Well, jump in. This is becoming no place for you.'

Robert sat down and put his arm affectionately round his father. He felt beautifully, happily safe once again. The Major, grinding the gears, inching the car out of the crowd, sniffed. 'Curnow must be supplying whisky to the Wazambas wholesale,' he said. 'I can smell it here.'

Chapter II

A NUMBER OF PEOPLE

I

Mr C. C. Yang lay on his camp bed. Count Curnow sat by him, looking with melancholy satisfaction at the neat job he had made of shaving a patch of hair from Yang's head and securing, with adhesive tape, a pad of lint over the contusion.

'Are you well enough to move?' asked the Count.

Mr Yang's eyes flickered about nervously. 'Please?' he said.

The Count, with awful distinctness, repeated his question.

'Oh yes. Very well, you know. But where are we going? Where are we to move to?'

'You are moving into my hut and I am moving into yours. I think it should be you who has to bear the constant smell of whisky.'

'Oh yes. Very nice,' said Yang, more nervous than ever. The Count had not yet uttered one word of reproach about the episode of the lost whisky.

'Please arrange for everything to be moved by this afternoon,' said the Count.

Mr Yang willed with all his soul that the gigantic bulk of

the Count would go quickly from his side: he felt oppressed and sweating, as though the Count were a dreadful spectre.

'Are you sure that it was the two boys you saw?' asked the Count.

'Yes. I think I am sure. I was hazy, you know. Hit on the head.'

'And they were quite alone?'

'Oh yes. I think so.'

The Count coughed. Even the cough was terrible.

'You will go back to Moru,' asked Mr Yang, 'and get more whisky?'

The Count grinned amiably. 'Even supposing cases of whisky were available in Moru, I could not afford to be away from here five days, you imbecile.'

II

Sete's aunt, reclining as usual on her veranda, sneezed. Immediately, she took a little wooden amulet, shaped like a forked radish, which was hanging round her neck, and thrust it up her nostrils, in order to stop any further portion of her soul escaping. It was like this that Sete found her when, with a few of his counsellors and warriors, he came to visit her, as he often did in the cool of the twilight. Seeing the amulet, Sete requested his aunt's soul to be whole and at peace with itself. She unplugged her nose, and smiled at him with affection. Sete sat down opposite her.

'Bring some of the powerful drink sent by the white man-fat-as-a-Wazamba-woman,' Sete's aunt commanded one of her attendant boys. The boy danced away like a cherub.

He returned in a few seconds. 'There is none left, madam,' he piped.

Sete's aunt frowned, and carefully avoided looking at her nephew. She was, however, perfectly aware that no more was left of the supply of whisky which Sete had passed on to her from the Count.

The effect of this passage was to make Sete assume an even more regal bearing. He had had no whisky from the Count now for three days. His aunt knew this, and he knew that she knew it.

'When I am given some I shall send you half,' said Sete.

'He who has nothing can afford to be generous,' replied Sete's aunt, quoting a Wazamba proverb, and turning upon the king at that moment the force of her rather protuberant eyes.

Sete squirmed uncomfortably on the mats. Only from his aunt, who had nursed him as a baby and seen into his heart at all the stages of his youth, would he have permitted such an insolent remark. Rather ostentatiously, he adjusted a square of red velvet which he was wearing round his shoulder.

This gesture was not lost on his aunt. 'That is a good piece of cloth,' she remarked.

'The fat man sent it me today.'

'However,' went on Sete's aunt, casually, 'it has neither the rarity nor the value of the drink.'

The king had already, in his most inward thoughts, half despised the gift of the cloth, and his aunt's observation was bitter to him.

'It is a good piece of cloth,' he said.

'Yes,' said his aunt. Her fat body was perfectly still, and she gazed beyond Sete towards the mountains whose dark grey peaks seemed, in the last hour of the day, very near.

She said thoughtfully: 'Brown is a good man. He does not change. He is a very good man and one to be trusted.'

Sete looked at his aunt with admiration. From the tangle of his conflicting motives and ideas and desires, she had given voice to the one notion in which he realized he believed.

'You are a wise woman,' he said.

She cackled and rapped one of her attendant cherubs over the head with a little stick she kept for that purpose.

'To be a king is difficult,' Sete continued. 'The life of a king is a continual crisis which those who are not kings do not often see.'

'There is a very great crisis now in the lives of the Wazambas, which everyone can see who is not an idiot,' his aunt remarked. 'The new times will be difficult and cruel, and the old times will never come again.' She rolled off her elbow on to her back. 'When I was a little girl, my grandfather said to me: "White men have arrived at the Lake; I pity you that you are young, and congratulate myself on being old." Well, old people hear the cry of a rhinoceros in the breaking of a twig, and imagine catastrophes near that are really far away; but I feel like my grandfather felt, all the same.'

In spite of her pessimism, so many of the veils of doubt and indecision were lifted in Sete's mind that he felt suddenly very happy.

'I have a little of the fat man's stimulant left,' he confessed. 'I will send for it.'

His aunt sat up with an astonishingly agile movement, and smoothed down her toga.

'Let us make the most of the times,' she said, 'which are neither old nor new, and which, like all times, have their pleasures and their pains.'

III

'Sete has been sober for three days,' Major Brown said.

Mr Craig tried to stop a yawn, keeping his mouth closed until his eyes watered. 'I hope that means something.'

'Either the Count's whisky has run out, or he is black-mailing Sete by withholding supplies,' said Dr Maine.

'I think the whisky has run out,' said Charles, with such obvious emphasis and so crude a wink, that Robert nearly jumped out of his skin. The double meaning, however, seemed lost on the rest of the party.

Everyone was more or less suppressing his irritability and nervousness at the long and so far fruitless negotiations with Sete. The Major and Dr Maine had been every day to the palace, waiting for hours in the stifling huts, arguing with and humouring Sete, joking with his aunt, trying to find out from her and Tetu and the king himself how much progress the Count had made, eating (out of politeness) endless stodgy maize cakes, drinking gallons of the frightful Wazamba beer. Some days Sete was amiable and seemed about to agree the terms proposed by Dr Maine's company (which he had at last been persuaded to hear); on other days he was sullen and suspicious; and frequently he would not see anyone, and would send out the grotesque priest (a boring old fraud) to undo any spells the white men might be casting over him, and to draw many red herrings across Maine's path.

'Nothing, *nothing* can ever be done in this country,' Dr Maine would cry, as they walked back to camp; but he would return to the attack the next day. He had infinite will power. The Major, long used to the coloured races' imperfect sense of the value of time, never betrayed any impatience: his brown eyes looked out of his leather-coloured face with only scientific emotion as he spoke soothingly to the chief Wazambas, and occasionally set down their behaviour in his note-book.

Mr Craig had put off and put off his return to Makala – at first through courtesy and to avoid breaking up the expedition, and later through sheer bad temper and a determination to see the thing through to the bitter end. He grumbled and was heavily sarcastic, and suffered dreadfully through eating the camp food, which though adequate was not dainty. But after breakfast – which now consisted for him of a plate of *posho* from the pot prepared for themselves by William, Joseph, and Mgambe – when his pipe was well going he was at his best, and told Mgambe to keep the rifles in first-class condition, and prophesied trouble with the Count's gang or the Wazambas or both. 'We shall have a little war on our hands in the end,' was his usual phrase. 'I suppose I had better stay and see it through. My presence will make our side of it more or less legal, anyway.'

Since the night of the dance Robert and Charles had been exceptionally well behaved; had never moved out of camp without one of the adults, or pleaded to go to the palace. Mr Craig said they were both sickening for malaria: the Major thought they were hatching a plot, and kept his anthropological eye on them.

'Well,' said the Major, 'whether the whisky has run out now or not, it will run out in time, and virtue will come into its own.'

'Hem,' said Mr Craig.

'Are you ready to go, Brown?' Dr Maine asked, standing up and placing his hat on his head in a comic way for the benefit of Robert.

The Major said he was, and in the everlasting sunshine they walked together down the now loathedly familiar slope to the town.

IV

In a far corner of the Wazamba country, among the foothills of the great mountains which are enveloped in damp mists sometimes all morning, and where the nights are chill, a young man sat outside his hut wrapped in furs and with a fur cap on his head. In the grey light the yellow blossoms on the trees shone with a penetrating and unearthly radiance. The young man had an ugly face, the bony structure of his forehead and cheeks projecting in curious humps. Opposite him squatted an old man so toothless and wrinkled that it looked as though a huge hand had taken his face and squeezed it together. He wore a short sheepskin which revealed the fact that his buttocks were wrinkled as well.

On the moist red earth in front of him, the old man had arranged a number of pots and seven little shells. Like a small girl playing at house, he was pouring water from one pot to another and then on the shells and occasionally on the young man's fingers which were stretched towards him. He had a cow's horn on which from time to time he rubbed the shells, and some dried cow dung which he made into a paste with water, and stuffed into his ears. This apparently meaningless performance was executed very slowly and deliberately, and seemed endless. While the old man fiddled about and mumbled, the young man looked patiently and impassively out from under his overhanging brow.

'O Lugu,' said the old man, at last, 'make your wish now.'

The young man closed his eyes, and wished to be king of the Wazambas.

The old man took the cow dung out of his ears and poured

the water from all the pots over the shells. He lifted the shells, around which the water had left a pattern on the earth, and placed them in one of the pots. He bent over and examined the pattern carefully and then looked up at Lugu.

'The wish will be fulfilled,' pronounced the old man.

Chapter 12

THE AGREEMENT

I

EARLY one morning, as the expedition sat at breakfast, William Kapaki came running up in a sweat of excitement, and released a flood of Swahili at Major Brown.

The Major put his plate on the grass and rose in a hurry. 'William says Curnow and Yang – the whole shooting-match – are moving off.'

'Rubbish,' said Mr Craig, but he was already standing up.

Everyone moved outside the circle of tents and looked down towards the town. Nothing unusual could be seen. All looked at William.

'There, there!' William said, pointing higher up the hill.

They ran up the slope in a body. From this point the guest huts and the palace buildings could be seen. Beyond the palisade, in two clouds of dust, were two motor cars, moving away from the town, but already too far off to be seen clearly by the naked eye. Robert had grabbed the telescope on his way out of camp and now passed it quickly to his father. The Major looked through it.

'William's right,' he exclaimed, handing it back to Robert. 'Very good, William, very good indeed.'

William grinned. Robert trained the telescope on the cars. In the front one it was just possible to identify the little splash of white as the Count: in the rear one there was quite definitely a sun-helmet with a feather in it. Charles, who was at Robert's ear, trying to peep down the telescope, whispered: 'What a triumph for *us*!'

'Bless my soul!' cried Mr Craig. 'Have we won the day?'

'Too soon to say,' modestly replied the Major, who could not, however, conceal the satisfaction he felt at this evidence of success in his long battle with the Count. 'It certainly looks as though Curnow has given up – which doesn't necessarily mean, of course, that we can now get an agreement with Sete. But it helps – tremendously.'

'That's an understatement,' Dr Maine said. 'But I don't believe in the Count's departure. It is too good to be true. He *never* gives up.'

Mr Craig had a thought which made him shudder violently. 'Suppose it's Curnow who has won the day? That he's going off because his job here is done, because *he* has got the agreement with Sete?'

'Likely,' said Dr Maine, mournfully. 'Much more likely.'

The Major bristled militarily. 'Don't agree. But we can soon find out the truth. We'll go along, Maine, and see Sete. Now.'

Leaving their breakfasts, they once more set off down the hill. Mr Craig and the two boys watched them until they were out of sight among the huts of the town.

Mr Craig appeared to be thinking deeply. 'I shall be greatly daring,' he said, at last, 'and have another cup of coffee. My nerves are a little on edge.'

II

The Count's exit appeared to have had no effect inside the palisade. The palace inhabitants were moving about as lazily as the sacred cows, though with more self-control. Tetu appeared.

'The guest huts are empty, I see,' said the Major.

Tetu made a bowing movement with his head, and looked pleased.

'We desire an audience with the king.'

Tetu tottered off to arrange it. He came back in half an hour and said that Sete's aunt would like to see them.

'But what about the king?' asked Major Brown.

Tetu said that Sete was engaged with his Rain Maker, and would not appear all day. The Major fumed, but knew that this was a good excuse if it were true. Among the Wazambas, the Rain Maker was a personage second only in importance to Sete. They went to see the aunt.

She was lying in her usual place on the veranda, eating maize cakes and bananas, and was delighted to see them. With her mouth full she asked indistinctly after the health of every member of the expedition in turn. They asked politely after her own. She described in detail the progress of a pain which had started in her right shin, travelled to her left shoulder and had finally settled in her stomach. Some small evil spirit – perhaps the ghost of a baboon – had clearly, she said, got into her body – probably through sleeping with her mouth open. Luckily she was now able, in its present situation, to appease it by sending down some food; which accounted for the cakes and fruit at this curious hour of the morning.

This was interesting, but they wanted news. Major Brown started to ask her about the relations between Sete and the Count. She seemed not to hear him. How were these unimportant but troublesome evil spirits dealt with in Major Brown's country? she asked. The Major opened his mouth to reply, but she ran on.

'I know,' said Sete's aunt, signing to one of her boys to remove the remains of her meal, and guffawing when she tripped him up with her rapping-stick as he went away, 'that you have certain liquids and powders, Brown, which you rub on the part where the evil spirit is, or which you swallow – and these, as I have observed when you used them on various of our people when you were here before, are very powerful. But what means do you employ to try to prevent the spirits lodging in the body at all?'

Major Brown groaned inwardly, and said the white man believed that illness and pain were not caused by evil spirits at all, but by small organisms present in the body or the air called, in English, *microbes*. Consequently the white man attacked the microbe, using drugs which would kill it but would not harm the body which it had infected.

Sete's aunt looked puzzled. 'But surely,' she said, 'there is only the difference of a word in our beliefs? This *microbe*, is it not the white man's word for evil spirit?'

The Major saw that Dr Maine was fidgeting and throwing up his eyes in prayer. 'No,' said the Major, finally, 'it is not.'

'Mm,' said Sete's aunt, very disappointed at this abrupt end to the conversation – there was nothing more she delighted in than such educational discussions – and casting about in her mind for a way to prolong it.

Before she could go on, Major Brown said: 'Has the king made an agreement with Curnow?'

Sete's aunt lay back on her cushions, and, opening her not very toothful mouth, laughed heartily. So heartily that even the Major and Dr Maine sniggered.

'She's a cunning old harridan,' said the Major, in English.

'What has all the conversation been about?' Maine asked.

'Rubbish.'

'Brown,' said Sete's aunt, when she had composed herself, 'underneath your kindness and quietness you are like all other white men. Material things – those are your real interests.'

'My dear madam,' said the Major, 'you know that in this matter I am merely speaking for my friend Maine.'

'Fiddle,' said Sete's aunt, amiably.

'And you haven't answered my question.'

'Well,' she said, 'if we are to come to the point so abruptly the answer is no.'

'And Curnow has gone away for good?'

'He has made no agreement with the king, and he has gone away. Whether he returns or not, I do not know.' She closed her eyes. 'For myself, I hope he returns – with a further supply of his strong drink,' she added, dreamily. She opened her eyes and cackled. '*That* was a powerful killer of microbes, eh?'

The Major told Maine the almost unbelievably excellent news.

'Now for Sete,' said Maine, polishing his dark glasses, and blinking happily.

'King Sete,' said Sete's aunt, suddenly, 'had a pain in his spear-arm, his right arm. Nothing our priests could do would remove it. A spy was sent to that village where Lugu, the king's wicked and ambitious brother, lives. There in the hut of an old magician the spy found a little image of Sete made out of clay. In the image's right arm was sticking a poisoned thorn. The spy removed the thorn and brought back the image. Sete's pain stopped. I find this very interesting. How is the microbe or evil spirit sent the great distance from Lugu's village to Sete's arm? Is the microbe first of all in the arm of the image? What is the connexion between the two arms?'

As she asked these somewhat difficult questions, Sete's aunt leaned forward earnestly, turning her head first to Major Brown and then to Dr Maine, holding them with her eye like the Ancient Mariner. The Major sighed, and settled himself more comfortably for the long philosophical conversation that now approached with the fateful inevitability of the Eumenides.

III

The same day, after Major Brown and Dr Maine had returned to camp, Sete, through Tetu, surprisingly requested them to see him. The Major refused. With the Count's departure he was feeling on firmer ground, and was delighted to drop the pleading attitude towards Sete which he had only taken up for Dr Maine's sake. 'It is now Sete's turn,' he said, 'to be on tenterhooks. Let him sit and think a little of how much he has to lose by not concluding an agreement with your company,

Maine.' He told Tetu that they would go to the palace the next day.

Early the following morning, Tetu was at the camp with a retinue of boys bearing an abundance and variety of good food such as had never been given the expedition before. He came also with an invitation for the party to move into the guest huts, which Major Brown, in spite of a lively protest from Mr Craig, refused. 'We can now be dignified,' said the Major, 'as befits our position. To refuse the Count's leavings will make an excellent impression on Sete.'

In the afternoon, the Major, Dr Maine, and Mr Craig, attended by William Kapaki, went to the palace. They took with them the second lion skin and a rich purple dressing-gown as presents for Sete, and to show their magnanimity. With Sete were the Rain Maker, the priest, all his counsellors, and a good selection of warriors. The party was received promptly and graciously: the Major was permitted to come to the point right away: a translation of the agreement between Sete and the African Gold Company was read, and, with hardly any discussion, Sete made his mark at the foot of the document, witnessed by Mr Craig. In half an hour it was all over. Dr Maine's company had the rights for ninety-nine years to the Wazamba gold.

At the celebratory dinner back in camp everything was talked over a score of times.

'It is clear now,' said the Major, 'that we were winning the race with Curnow even when we thought we were marking time. All during our long wait, our unsatisfactory interviews with Sete, Curnow must have made no progress at all, in spite of his whisky. The whisky, in fact, merely persuaded Sete to see him, and when it gave out Curnow must have been shown pretty obviously that he was distrusted – I told you all, you remember, long ago that Sete distrusted most white men – and so he gave up. Sete's aunt helped us, too, I believe. The king takes notice of what she says, and she likes us and sees that we are honest.'

Dr Maine said: 'I owe everything to you, Brown – not only to your patient and tactful negotiations but also because I was able to tell Sete that you would stay here after the company starts operations, and look after the Wazambas' welfare. And I can never be too grateful to Craig, who stuck it out so well, and who gave us our semi-official status, and whose stomach is not ruined beyond repair, I hope.'

'I am sure there is a little moral in all this for you two boys,' said Mr Craig, as he picked a chicken bone. 'We thought we were doing vilely and it turns out we were doing well. Precisely what the moral is I leave you to guess – I cannot.'

The two boys, who knew much but said nothing, grinned.

Chapter 13

THE DRUMS

ROBERT was almost sorry as the preparations were made for their departure. However tedious or unpleasant their experiences in a place, some people always regret having to leave it, and Robert was one of them. The snow-capped peak and the swift river, the site of the camp and the palace, Tetu and Sete's aunt, had all made a deep impression on him; and by contrast the dingy shops and streets of Makala seemed to hold out promise of nothing but dullness.

Major Brown and William Kapaki were to stay behind with one of the cars until Dr Maine had been to South Africa to report to his company: it was thought that a continuous watch should be kept on things in the Wazamba country. Mr Craig, of course, was long over-due in Makala, and Robert and Charles would soon have to be back at school. Robert was going to live with the Craigs until school started.

On the day after the agreement with Sete, by the time everything was packed, and the Major's belongings and the necessary stores had been moved to one of the guest huts (where he had, at Sete's insistence, agreed to live), it was well on into the afternoon and Dr Maine and Mr Craig decided to delay their setting-out until the following morning. After tea, when the temperature had gone down a little, Robert and Charles went for a walk along the river valley.

'It's hard to imagine that only a few weeks have gone since I said good-bye to old Dobbin,' Robert remarked, thoughtfully.

'Who on earth is old Dobbin?' asked Charles.

'The headmaster of my school in England. He had a face like a horse, and yellow teeth.'

'How curious! The head of the school you are going to attend in Africa has a face like a horse,' said Charles. 'But his teeth aren't yellow. A greyish green, I should say. An impressive figure, though.'

'My father has always told me never to be impressed by schoolmasters – or intimidated, either. He says no man ought to get as much respect and discipline as a schoolmaster gets.'

'Still,' said Charles, 'there is no doubt that some people *are* impressive, however much you decide in your own mind that they shouldn't be. Look at the Count.'

'Well, the Count is an exception. What is sinister and terrifying about the Count is that he doesn't seem to have any weaknesses or desires that you can appeal to. He just goes on with his job and has no other real interests. It wouldn't hurt him even if you killed his chameleon. I don't see how you *could* hurt him. He's absolutely invulnerable. Now Maine is an example of a bogus impressive figure, like old Dobbin – except that Dr Maine is nice and sincere and Dobbin was nasty and hypocritical. If Dr Maine is impressive at all, he is impressive in an ordinary way, like you or my father or William Kapaki – just because he has ordinary virtues.'

They came to a pool into which the river dropped in a short, shining curtain and became still and black before pouring out again. The steep sides of the pool were damp: these and the vegetation on its brink made the place dark, with vague globules of light flickering on ferns and rock. When one looked up, the sky was strangely high. It seemed as though there were no human beings in existence except themselves. There was no noise except of the continuous falling of water into water. Robert felt his scalp creep.

'This is impressive,' said Charles.

'Isn't it? I wonder why,' said Robert. 'Perhaps we lived here in a previous existence. Or shall do in a future one.'

'I don't believe in future existences. Or past ones, for that matter. Perhaps something exciting is going to happen here.'

As they watched they could hear, beneath the rapid drumming of the water, another drumming, much slower, further off and yet distinct. They looked at one another.

'Do you hear anything?' asked Charles.

Robert said he did, and with one accord they began to scramble up the side of the valley. Low trees got in their way. Avoiding them they encountered a clump of fleshy, light green cacti. Circumnavigating the cacti they had to trudge through waist-high grass. From under Robert's feet a black snake suddenly uncoiled itself and threshed away through the grass.

'Oh-h-h!' shouted Robert, in the tone of one having a nightmare, and started running in the opposite direction, raising his knees ludicrously high, as though he were doing some physical exercise. Charles laughed until he could not walk, and sank to the ground. Robert came up cautiously, very offended.

'You wouldn't have behaved much better, I bet.'

'I'm not saying I should,' said Charles. 'But that doesn't mean you looked less funny.'

'It was the first snake I'd ever seen in Africa. Was it poisonous?'

'Don't know. It wriggled away as though you were.'

'Very amusing,' said Robert. 'I'll race you to the top.'

They came out panting on to the high ground above the waterfall and pool. Immense green distances lay about them. The drumming they had heard below was here more distinct. It came from a place much further than the town.

'What is it?' said Robert. 'Another dance?' As soon as he had made this remark, a strange feeling of dread seized him, quite without reason. It was as though he knew positively that the drums were sounding for a reason not innocent, but menacing.

Charles did not appear to be disturbed: he had thrown himself down on the grass and now lay on his back watching a buzzard which in the still air above them hovered on motionless wings.

'Might be,' he replied lazily. 'Probably someone is dead. Africans have processions and make a great deal of noise when anyone dies, to frighten away the dead man's spirit which might be lingering.'

Again, Robert felt an unreasonable fear, and thought for a stupid second that it was his father who might be dead. He sat down beside Charles, wishing, but not daring, to voice his uneasiness.

'Shall we go back?' he said, at length.

Charles' eyes were closed. 'The modern groglidon is abstemious,' he said, thickly.

Robert gave him a severe poke. 'Charles! Charles! You're going to sleep.'

Charles opened his eyes vaguely. 'Nonsense,' he said, 'I'm wide awake.'

'Come on. Let's go back.'

'Oh dear!' Charles yawned, and got to his feet.

When they were not far from camp they saw the bright figure of William Kapaki. He waved his ostrich-head stick, and came running towards them.

'*Bwana* Brown says hurry,' he said respectfully but firmly.

'What's the matter, William?' said Robert, who was still anxious.

As William replied, a drum very near them started to sound urgently and monotonously. This one certainly was in the town.

'There is a war between the Wazambas,' said William.

Chapter 14

A GLIMPSE OF WAR

I

THE Wazamba civil war of this period never got into the history books, though mention of it was made in a few volumes of memoirs – notably, in one called *A Chequered Life* by Algernon Maine, which appeared much later and sold forty-three copies. It was, in fact, one of those brief, obscure wars, with a profound but not obviously direct effect on the history of the region in which it was fought. In the great development of the Wazamba country during the years which followed it, it was completely forgotten.

The drums which Robert and Charles had heard in the far distance were Lugu's drums. This much Major Brown was able to tell them when they hurried into camp that memorable evening. Tetu had come with the news from King Sete, and the news had come to Sete in that curious African way of spreading information which was partly by a deliberate espionage system, partly by gossip and rumour. Tetu was still being questioned, but he had nothing much to add to his original bare statement. Joseph and Mgambe were lighting a fire: in the half-darkness the light from the growing flames flickered eerily on the green canvas of the tents, on the cars, the lenses of Major Brown's spectacles, on Tetu's nut-like skull and fringe of white wool.

Lugu was two hours' march away with at least a hundred warriors – that was what Tetu's knowledge boiled down to. He was trying to keep an impassive exterior but he was clearly very distressed. Robert, too, was distressed, with emotions he could hardly explain to himself. For Tetu, standing there so ancient and vulnerable, and for all the Wazambas, he felt an overwhelming embarrassment. It was as though a disgraceful secret which they had so far hidden behind their normal activities had suddenly been revealed; as though the war, some huge legendary beast, had burst the chains with which they had weighted it down, and had risen irresistibly, breaking the calm surface of life with its rotten hulk. And Robert felt as well, quite illogically, that he and all the expedition were as responsible as the Wazambas for the war.

At length Tetu departed. Major Brown sat down rather wearily in his camp chair. 'We must all move to the guest hut, I think. Lugu is burning villages and killing male prisoners, and might not stop at white men. We shall be able to protect ourselves better in the huts if it comes to that – though I don't think it will.'

Mr Craig was utterly appalled at the state the Wazambas had got into. 'The British Government should have taken the country over ten years ago. I've always said so. Now we shall have to get that company of *askaris*. I suggest that one of us takes a car, and Robert and Charles, and dashes to Makala at once.'

'I agree,' said the Major. 'Robert and Charles must be got out of this as soon as possible, and Makala must be informed. And, also, some of us must stay here and see the thing to the end. Apart from trying to keep Sete on the throne and safeguarding Maine's agreement, we have a clear responsibility to use our influence to make peace.'

There was then a tremendous argument between the three men as to who should take the car and the boys to Makala. Dr Maine and the Major were convinced that it should be Mr Craig: Mr Craig was equally certain that it was his duty to stay and see the war through, and not to run away. The boys joined in, too, and protested against being made to behave like rats on a sinking ship. All to no avail – it was firmly settled in the end that Mr Craig should take the car and the boys as soon as it was light the following morning.

Mr Craig consoled himself. 'Of course, by then Lugu may have cut all our throats.'

They began the tedious job of moving all their belongings to the guest huts. It was pandemonium in the town. The female, aged, and infant inhabitants were engaged in moving, too: loaded with pots, food, cloth, mats, and leading their cattle, they were leaving their huts and making for the safety of the forest. The moonlight gleamed on wide, frightened eyeballs, and the choking dust, which their feet had raised, glittered and swirled. From within the palisade, where Sete's warriors were massing, came the flickering of fires, the beating of many drums, and regular, but sometimes confused, shouting. Once, a patrol of twenty young men with spears, bodies and faces painted white and gashed red, their mouths open and roaring, dashed through the town, scattering children, cows, household belongings. To Robert they seemed real with a reality he had hardly known in his life before, and he was stricken with the thought that these youths were going out into the dark and limitless African spaces to kill and be killed.

At last the expedition was lodged completely in the guest huts. Dr Maine, Mr Craig, and the Major arranged to keep watch in turn throughout the night. Tetu was to keep them informed of the course of events. The guns were loaded, the ammunition stacked ready. There seemed nothing more of any use to be done, and the boys were packed off to bed.

They were in the middle hut, in the very room once occupied by the Count. A reminiscent odour hung about. With this in his nostrils, and the noise from the palace and the streets, Robert thought he would be awake all night. 'I shall never sleep,' he said to himself, pulling the sheet over his ears, and the next thing he knew was that William Kapaki was nudging his shoulder gently and that the morning sun was streaming through the window and making a bright patch on the mud floor.

'So we haven't all had our throats cut,' Robert remarked, springing out of bed.

Charles was yawning. 'Well, I don't know about the others, but mine is all right.'

II

Everyone was all right. As they gathered for breakfast on the veranda of one of the huts, Robert noticed how very normal they all looked, and he could not help feeling that the confusion and excitement of the night was simply a dream. Outside the veranda the roadway was deserted: nothing came from the palisade except blue threads of smoke from domestic fires. And then the old Dodge, driven by Joseph, pulled up in front of the hut: it was ready to take them away, and Robert gazed at it with sadness.

'I don't like leaving you,' he said suddenly to his father.

'No need to worry,' said the Major, in a gruff voice. 'Come on, have a good breakfast: long journey ahead of you.'

Robert could eat nothing. With a very sickly feeling he listened to them discussing the war.

'Naturally,' said the Major, 'Lugu's rebellion has been possible ever since the death of the old king.'

'What I am worried about,' remarked Mr Craig, facetiously, 'is that Lugu will win the war, and that we shall have to come back here and negotiate all over again for a mining concession.'

But no one laughed, and Mr Craig hastily returned to his *posho*. Robert kept looking at the gate in the palisade, hoping that Tetu would come through it and bring them the news that Sete's men had beaten off Lugu's, that the war was over. There had been little news during the night. Major Brown had been to the palace and had found out that, so far as was known, Lugu was still a good many miles off, in the north, and that the way to Makala, which lay to the south-west, was open and not threatened. The Major had checked this infor-

mation by interviewing the messengers who had come in to
Sete from the front. He was more worried about sending
Robert off to Makala than Robert was about leaving his father
here. But the risk of encountering the rebels on the journey
had to be taken: it was a smaller risk than that of Lugu penetrating to and even capturing the capital.

Of the possible danger on the road Robert had no realiza-
tion: he climbed into the back seat of the Dodge, among the
tents and tins of bully beef, with no emotion other than sadness. Mr Craig took his foot suddenly off the clutch; the car
jerked forward; Mr Craig changed into second gear with a
horrible grinding sound, and the guest huts began to recede.
To Robert, the group standing in front of them, waving
good-bye, seemed charged with pathos. His father and Dr
Maine stood together; the Major had a pipe in his mouth, his
legs came out of his khaki shorts with the symmetry and
solidity of those of a billiard table. By contrast, Maine looked
especially wispy as he flapped a pale hand, his hat alone
having any reality – the reality of a rather queer-shaped
chimney pot. Mgambe and Joseph were squatting as usual
but waving nevertheless. The whiteness of William's grin
could be seen long after many details of the scene were
blurred by distance.

The Dodge entered the forest. Rattling over the track in
the gloom under the trees, with Charles singing in a loud and
tuneless voice, Robert felt a pang of apprehension. He could
not have given a name to what he feared, but the whole scene
seemed suddenly unreal. He could see Mr Craig's profile, the
jaws working as he sucked a magnesia tablet. The butterflies
drifted upwards in front of the car as they had done that evening of the expedition's arrival.

'*And she died through drinking a mouse in her beer,*' sang
Charles.

'Oh, shut up!' cried Robert.

Charles looked round, very surprised. 'All right, if you
don't like it.'

They proceeded in silence.

It was a long time before they reached the end of the forest.

The track out of it led up a slope. As the trees gave way to grass the Dodge put on speed; so much speed that as it topped the hill Mr Craig, with its decrepit brakes, could not prevent it running down the other side. He would have liked to stop it dead, for against the green of the landscape, in three vivid places, were red springing flames and columns of heavy smoke, which came from three burning villages.

III

The nearest could not have been at a greater distance than a quarter of a mile. Mr Craig and the boys gazed at them in paralysed fascination. And then the significance of them sunk into their minds. At the same time they saw about thirty Negroes, wearing tall head-dresses and carrying spears and shields, running towards them from the fires. Cries from the warriors came faintly but clearly over the distance.

Without a word Mr Craig began fumbling with the gear lever of the Dodge.

'Lugu's men, of course,' muttered Charles, at last.

'Of course,' said Mr Craig.

The turning round of the car was like an incident in a nightmare when urgent fears can only be translated into slow and gluey action. The hollows of the slope prevented a simple semicircle being made: Mr Craig had to back and edge forward, and back again. The gears ground like the teeth of a restless sleeper.

In the meantime, Lugu's warriors drew closer. Charles could contain himself no longer. 'For the Lord's sake, Father!' he cried, in a fret.

'This cannot be done any quicker,' said Mr Craig, with amazing calm. 'And I do not care for your language, Charles.'

Both the boys felt a rush of confidence in Mr Craig. Charles said: 'Sorry, Father.'

'Get down in your seats, you two,' said Mr Craig.

Robert was about to ask why when he saw, sailing through the air towards them, what looked like an umbrella. The umbrella fell and stuck into the ground ten yards away and quivered. It was a spear, with a ruff of straw dyed red round the haft near the point. Robert ducked. He had a curious wish to hide every square inch of his body behind something, even though it were only the folded canvas hood of the car.

Lugu's warriors were near enough for their grotesquely painted faces to be seen. Their shouts were bloodcurdling.

'Off we go,' said Mr Craig. The car was now pointing towards the forest, and it took a great leap forward to safety. Robert's heart leaped with it. As Mr Craig pressed the accelerator the swaying and bumping was fearful. The boys' fingers became numb with holding on. Mr Craig was hunched over the wheel like a jockey. Suddenly, the windscreen in front of him was shattered, and, almost simultaneously, they all heard a resounding *whee*.

'Good God!' exclaimed Mr Craig. 'The beggars have got rifles!'

There was then a number of shots in rapid succession. The toes of everyone in the car curled inwards in anxiety. Mr Craig pressed still harder on the accelerator, and if the car did not turn over it was not his fault. The boys were thrown about like a pea in a whistle.

And then, all at once it seemed, they were in the gloom of the forest, with the trees comfortingly thick about them. The shooting stopped. The shouting died away. The car jolted on in comparative silence. They all started talking together.

'Are we going back to the guest huts?' asked Robert, when they had sorted their questions out.

'We are indeed,' said Mr Craig, grimly. 'And not only for our own welfare: the others must be warned quickly that Lugu is coming from the south-west – instead of (or as well as) the north. Lugu is far more dangerous than anyone thought – you see how speedily his men reacted to our presence? They shot at us not because we menaced them, but because they knew if we escaped we should give their plan of campaign away.'

'There seemed to be so few of them,' said Charles. 'And the villages were burning so casually. And then we came along so accidentally. I had imagined a war to be very different. There is such a lot of space where the war *isn't*.'

Chapter 15

THE LETTER

I

NEITHER was the return of the Dodge as Charles had imagined it. Instead of Major Brown and the others rushing in amazement and alarm out of the guest huts, volleying questions at them about their reappearance, about the broken windscreen, they found the whole place utterly deserted. They climbed out of the car, hot, tired and with raging headaches. They looked in all the huts.

'Lugu has carried them off,' remarked Mr Craig, satirically.

'You don't really think anything bad has happened to them, do you?' Robert asked, a little anxiously.

Mr Craig shook his little grey head. 'They are probably having lunch with Sete. Or bathing. They don't seem to realize that there is a war on.'

Charles, mooching round the back of the huts, found Joseph fast asleep in the shade. Charles prodded him. He got up with a guilty grin. On being questioned, he said that everyone else had gone inside the palisade.

'Come along, boys,' said Mr Craig. 'Let us see what goes on there.'

They went through the gates. It was very quiet. A few old men tottered about among the cows. They found the Major and the others on the veranda of the hut belonging to Sete's aunt. Their appearance caused a sensation but they were now too weary to appreciate it. Mr Craig related concisely the events which had driven them back.

'Rifles!' exclaimed Major Brown. 'I can't understand that. Even Sete, with far more power and wealth than Lugu, has no fire-arms at all.'

'It seems to me that Lugu has a very good chance of winning this war. And what is the position then?' said Mr Craig.

'The Government must be persuaded to intervene on Sete's behalf,' said Dr Maine. 'In any case, my agreement is beginning to look sick. What my company will say to the bill for expenses I present them with and no results, I shudder to think.'

The Major then told Mr Craig what had happened in the town since the Dodge had left. Very early there had been a short but tremendous burst of shouting and drumming from the palisade. And then Sete had rushed out at the head of his army. He had gone in the direction in which his patrols had reported Lugu to be, namely, to the north. Sete's neat trousers and shirt had been laid aside; of all the warriors he was daubed the most grotesquely and fiercely. When he had gone, Tetu had come to the guest huts with a message from Sete's aunt, and so here they all were. The Rain Maker and the priest were with the army, Sete's wives were evacuated, but a few people still remained in the palisade.

Sete's aunt had been trying to persuade them to leave the guest huts and take up residence in the palace. She had put forward a number of powerful arguments in favour of this move. First, if Sete should be defeated or compelled to retreat, the palisade represented a far more formidable defence for Major Brown's expedition than the guest huts. Secondly, if the palisade had to be defended it was clearly better for the preparations to be made now, when the threat against it was not acute and they had plenty of time; and who better than the Major to make such preparations? Thirdly, by virtue of the agreement, Sete and Dr Maine were in close alliance; the success of the expedition in securing the Wazamba gold depended on the success of Sete against the rebels; the expedition could not stand aside and be neutral.

When the Major had finished telling them this, they all looked towards the end of the veranda where Sete's aunt lay in a black lump with her eyes shut, asleep or pretending to be.

'The woman's dead right,' exclaimed Mr Craig, 'I think.'

'I'm sure she is,' said Dr Maine, 'especially now we know that a section of Lugu's army is only beyond the forest. I don't think there is any time to lose.'

The Major was frowning, and visibly ill at ease. 'I don't like it,' he said, slowly but forcefully. 'Quite frankly, Maine, I don't care two pins about your agreement, and I am certain we have no moral right to defend it by force of arms. Our duty is obvious – by our actions not to be responsible for the injury of a single man in this rebellion; and, also, to inform the responsible authorities as soon as possible so that peace may be restored.'

Dr Maine tried to speak, but the Major went heavily on. 'Perhaps you think my principles a little theoretical,' he said, fixing the two other men in turn with a stubborn eye, 'but they are going to guide my actions all the same. If Lugu and his men appear I shall take steps to warn them that there are white men here, and then, if they attack, I shall defend our expedition. But I don't think they will attack. Lugu is not a fool, he knows that he dare not offend the white man's government. His only chance of succeeding in his revolt is a quick victory over Sete, and then, if our Government interferes, to demonstrate that he has the support of more of the Wazambas than Sete had.'

The Major looked sharply at them all, and then added: 'I am sure I am going to have your support in this.'

There was a long silence – a silence which took the place of argument. Dr Maine and Mr Craig felt it was too late for argument. The former sighed and pushed back his black hat.

'I think you are unrealistic, Brown, but I am with you, of course.'

'We shall all be murdered,' said Mr Craig, 'but our consciences will be clear, and so we shall float straight up to heaven. I agree very reluctantly.'

Major Brown then walked up to Sete's aunt, and told her that the expedition must remain neutral and in the guest huts. She sat up and looked at him sadly with her large brown eyes, but nodded and did not speak. It seemed as though she had known, from the start, what the Major's attitude would be. As they left her, lying there alone, she had such a pathetic, doomed look that Robert felt he might easily weep about her. He was very tired.

II

They were all tired, but back at the guest huts Major Brown made them work, nevertheless. His neutrality was an armed neutrality, and he directed that the hut nearest the palisade be made a strong point. All the arms and ammunition were brought into it, and what remained of the food as well. The Africans were sent to the river for a large supply of water. Empty packing cases – their own and those left behind by the Count – were filled with dry earth, and arranged round the window-openings inside the hut. The cars were driven close to the hut walls.

The hut commanded the entrance to the palisade and also the wide street which led through the centre of the town. From one window a clear view could be had up the slopes to the forest. When all the preparations had been completed, Joseph was told to brew some tea, and all the whites sat on the veranda sipping it while William Kapaki kept a watch on the forest. It was four o'clock. The sun was still hot and the air was calm, except that now and then a leaning dust-devil would come whirling along the street and dance away over the palisade. The town, with its abandoned huts, a stray dog panting in the shade, looked already conquered. The party on the veranda sipped gloomily.

Joseph squatted on the ground below them. In front of him he had a piece of broken mirror propped against a stone. He had found a pink ribbon on an empty drum of turkish delight, left behind by the Count, and was tying it in various positions on his black, curly head. At each new position he squinted at himself in the mirror in a pleased manner. Watching him, Robert again felt like weeping: Joseph, in his innocent ugliness and vanity, was far more pathetic than funny.

Mr Craig put down his cup, and wiped his lips delicately. 'I feel like an aristocrat in a tumbril,' he remarked.

No one made any reply to this. Major Brown had surrounded himself with a smoke-screen from his pipe. Dr Maine had surreptitiously opened Kierkegaard, and was reading guiltily with an air of not reading. Charles Craig was constructing a scientific fly-trap with the melted sugar in the dregs of his tea, his overturned tea-cup and a spoon. The minutes wore on.

'Or a man in a dentist's waiting-room,' said Mr Craig, suddenly.

The appearance of Lugu's warriors could hardly be longer delayed. Robert got up. 'I think I'll go and see what William is doing,' he said. No opposition being offered, he walked into the back room of the hut.

The window framed a picture of vivid greens backed by blue sky. William, wearing his flapped cap, stood looking out. He smiled when Robert came up to him, but did not turn his head.

'*Jambo*,' said Robert, with a view to airing his few words of Swahili.

'*Jambo*,' replied William, taking out of his mouth a huge cigarette he had rolled from a piece of newspaper.

'*Abari?*'

'*Mzuri.*'

'*Mzuri sana?*'

'*Ndio, bwana.*'

Robert, his Swahili exhausted with this exchange of 'hellos', lapsed into English.

'Have you seen anything?'

'*Hapana, bwana.*' At his own joke of continuing Swahili, William giggled in the falsetto voice he used for laughing.

Robert leaned on the earth-boxes and gazed out into the sunlight. William dropped the butt of his cigarette on the floor and extinguished it with his bare foot. Robert shuddered.

'William, you must have feet like a horse.'

William did not follow this conversational opening: his eyes, the shape of almonds, looked constantly out.

He said, quietly but vigorously: '*Bwana*, they are here.'

Robert went cold, and felt each separate hair on his scalp. 'Where, William? I can't see anything.'

But William had gone. Robert peered up the slope. Soon, he saw what looked like a white butterfly fluttering against the farthest trees. It was joined by another, and another. In a few moments there was a pattern of dancing white flecks, and then they clicked into shape and meaning, and he saw that they were the blanched feathered head-dresses of many warriors, and that they were coming down the slope. Dr Maine, carrying a rifle, joined him at the window.

'I bet five shillings they'll attack us,' said Robert, in a voice which, to his surprise, trembled.

'I shan't take you,' said Maine, leaning comfortably on the earth-boxes, and squinting through the sights of his rifle. 'Though your father, who really knows these people, says they will leave us alone.'

Robert went to look for the Major. Mr Craig and Mgambe were on the veranda, with rifles, but looking unconcerned. The Major was standing in the middle of the space between the hut and the palisade, facing the approaching warriors, his pipe between his teeth, his hands in his pockets. Robert restrained an impulse to run out and pull him back into the hut. He was a perfect target for rifle bullets, to say nothing of spears.

Robert went anxiously back to Dr Maine, so as to observe the approach of Lugu's men. It seemed to him that he might, by watching them, *will* them not to injure his father. He looked through the window. The butterflies had gone.

'What's happened?'

'They are out of sight,' said Dr Maine.

'Clearly.'

Dr Maine was amused at this piece of impudence. 'Sorry,' he said, 'if I'm not being explicit. They are behind an undulation of the hill – and have apparently stopped advancing.'

'Stopped! Are you sure that they're not outflanking us?'

Dr Maine's grin grew broader. 'Quite sure.'

Robert rushed out to his father. 'They're not coming,' he panted.

The Major removed his pipe. 'That is what it looks like to me, too,' he said. 'Now go back and calm down.'

Robert went back, feeling abashed. Events seemed to have a habit of not coming up to his expectations, of occurring very much more slowly than they ought. He stood on the veranda and watched, with disgust, Charles operating his fly-trap.

'Five flies in half an hour. Not very efficient,' remarked Charles.

'Don't be so blasé,' said Robert, and went in to Dr Maine again.

'It looks as though I should have lost my five bob,' said Robert.

'Don't be so impatient, my dear fellow. You must remember that the enemy is just as dubious about us as we are about him. We might go on for days watching each other.'

Robert began properly to appreciate the war's timing. He yawned. 'What about a tune on the flute, then?'

'If you pull my leg I shall complain to your father. Or better still, I *shall* play my flute.'

III

All the same, before night fell a number of curious and startling events had occurred. At five o'clock, the watchers in the hut observed a single figure emerge against the green background of the hill and start coming towards them. It was seen to be plumeless. Robert found the telescope, and used it. As he adjusted it, the woolly image jumped into focus and hit him between the eyes.

He had handed the telescope to his father (who by that time was back in the hut) before he was able to speak his one word.

'Yang!'

'Bless my soul!' exclaimed Mr Craig.

Dr Maine turned from the window, and looked long at the Major. 'I see,' he said, at last, 'that it's not much of a surprise to you.'

The Major coughed. 'No,' he admitted. 'I don't believe too much in coincidences.'

'You don't believe in coincidences, Father?' said Robert. 'What on earth do you mean?'

'He means,' said Maine, 'that Lugu's rebellion was far, far too convenient for Count Curnow.'

'Count Curnow!' repeated Robert, rather stupidly.

'Well,' said the Major, 'I must go out and receive Yang.'

Robert now wished that action could be postponed a little in favour of talk. He was not altogether clear about what was happening. But Yang walked on. He walked, Robert observed through the window, with a limp still, and a stick, and wore, instead of a hat, a bandage. He looked very small and very evil. Dr Maine kept him covered with a rifle. He passed the line of sight of the window, and by the time Robert had gone out to the veranda he had turned round and was limping back up the hill. Major Brown came to the hut carrying a letter.

'You let him go?' said Robert, in astonishment.

Major Brown shrugged his shoulders. 'What did you want me to do? Ask him in for a cup of tea?' He opened the letter. Everyone gathered round to read it.

Dear Major, (it said, in an angular writing which Robert remembered with a pang, and which brought the hot and squalid atmosphere of the Hotel Splendide around him in an instant), *My friend Lugu, King of the Wazambas, proposes to occupy his capital and palace at dawn tomorrow. I think you will wish to avoid unnecessary bloodshed, but, of course, I am not sure, and therefore write this note by way of warning and also by way of instruction. Kindly prepare, with all your party, to leave this country at first light tomorrow. My employee, Mr Yang, will accompany you, and his presence will ensure your safe con-*

duct through King Lugu's lines. Best regards to my young friend Robert. Sincerely yours, Hugo Curnow.

It was Mr Craig who broke the silence. 'The impudent scoundrel!' he cried.

Dr Maine did not speak: he felt keenly his position. Compliance with Curnow's letter would mean the utter failure of his mission to the Wazambas. On the other hand, defiance of it could not but involve them all in dangerous and complicated events.

Robert determined the course of the discussion. The light of understanding had slowly been flooding his brain, and he burst out: 'Those heavy cases in the Count's room must have been cases of rifles! He'd planned this all the time.'

'What heavy cases, Robert?' asked the Major, gently.

Too late Robert realized what he had given away. 'Those cases I saw when –'

'When?' asked the Major, encouragingly.

'When Charles and I went to the Count's hut and broke all his bottles of whisky,' he said in a gallop, knowing that it was useless to prevaricate. 'I'm sorry, Charles.'

'Bless my soul!' said Mr Craig, again.

Very soon Major Brown had the whole story. 'So you two boys were really responsible for the Count's departure,' he said.

'And the signing of my agreement,' Dr Maine said.

'And the war,' added Mr Craig, with a sigh.

Robert looked appalled. 'No, no. Not all that. Perhaps we just helped a bit to get your agreement through, Dr Maine, but we didn't – of course – intend anything else.'

Mr Craig, whose character seemed to Robert to have blossomed surprisingly in the rich Wazamba air, came over and dug him in the shoulder. 'Don't worry about it, young man. Even without your intervention things would inevitably have become unpleasant – as I forecast right at the start.'

'Was what we did very wrong?' asked Robert, generally. 'I mean apart from it being done secretly and so on.'

'Very wrong,' said Dr Maine, solemnly. 'Thank you both very much indeed.'

The Major had to smile, and the boys knew that even though they were not, perhaps, forgiven, they were excused. 'I shall speak to you both seriously when we have some leisure,' he said.

Mr Craig put on a grim face. 'We shall ignore Curnow's letter, naturally?'

'I'm glad,' said the Major, 'that you still feel belligerent, Craig. I know how Maine feels. For me, the whole situation has changed now that we know for certain that Lugu's revolt is not genuine. Lugu is merely Curnow's tool, or so it seems, and I am sure that he has even less general support among the Wazambas than I thought at first. If his following is small, then Sete should be back here very soon with his warriors, having dealt with it successfully. Our duty to the Wazambas and to ourselves is to deal in the meantime with Curnow and Yang. To surrender the capital to them means prolonging Sete's task of crushing the rebellion – an artificial rebellion – unnecessarily. I propose that we go behind the palisade and defend it.'

The Major made this speech slowly and awkwardly, but it did not represent the half of what he felt. He was changing his views only with much heart-searching and heart-burning. No line of conduct he could possibly advocate then seemed to him to have any virtue. His life, previously always so simple, he had tangled disastrously.

Chapter 16

BEHIND THE PALISADE

I

'WHAT reply are you going to make to the Count?' Robert asked his father, privately, during a convenient interval in the ensuing discussion.

'None,' said Major Brown.

Robert shuddered. He alone of the party, it seemed to him, had an accurate idea of the Count's power and resource and ruthlessness. He even imagined that in some occult way the Count was able to hear their plans for countering his request to them to depart; that the plans were stupid and useless. He had the old sense that the Count was toying with them.

So that Robert joined with a strange feeling of unreality in the work which had to be done. Since the party was, without doubt, being watched from the hill, the move to the palisade was to be made when it was completely dark, but before the moon had risen. That was not a long time. The sun was down already: the green silk of the sky was blackening. Within the huts all the stores were made ready to be rushed to the cars when such an operation would pass unnoticed from a distance.

The new situation was explained to William Kapaki and

Mgambe: their active help would be needed if it actually came to a pitched battle for the palace. Joseph's simple mind was not thought capable of appreciating the turn of events, and the sudden move behind the palisade was left to be interpreted by him as a fresh example of the eccentricity and the pointless, demoniac energy of the white races. He could not, anyway, use a rifle. With the pink ribbon now tied round his neck, he looked like a fattish, black (and cross-eyed) cat. He helped to fold the beds once more, however, with a willing air, and broke only two plates when packing the crockery.

The stars came out. The frogs by the river started their rasping. The cars were loaded quickly. Major Brown, his face glistening with sweat, came to Dr Maine, who was still keeping watch by the window.

'Ready,' he said. Dr Maine was to drive the Ford van, as before, Mr Craig the Dodge, and the Major his own car: the Major was to lead the procession, Dr Maine to bring up the rear. Though all the details had been carefully settled, the plan in practice, like all plans, became a little confused. As the party hurriedly and silently squeezed into the cars, among the bully beef and petrol cans, Charles Craig, who should have gone with his father, found himself without a place. Joseph, whose amiable but blank face could be perceived in the darkness through the front window of the Dodge, was clearly the spanner in the works – a spanner firmly wedged, and settling itself down for a long drive.

'Come in with me,' whispered Dr Maine into Charles' ear. Charles crept back with Maine to the Ford and crawled in the back over the piled camp beds. He could see, past Dr Maine's hat (the shape of something on the boiler of an early locomotive), the dim outlines of the cars in front, and beyond, the dark line of the palisade against a sky already beginning to glow a ruddy orange with the rising moon. The cars started to move away. Dr Maine pressed cautiously on the Ford's self-starter.

Nothing happened. Dr Maine jabbed it violently. There was no response. He turned round to Charles with a grimace, and then got out and lifted up the seat. He scrabbled in the tool-box for the starting handle, making what seemed to Charles a noise fit to bring on them a million rebellious Wazamba tribesmen.

'Can I help?' hissed Charles. Dr Maine shook his head, held up the starting handle triumphantly, and ran round to the front of the Ford. The other cars had disappeared. Somewhere, a night bird emitted two eerie calls. Charles began to feel that the isolation of the Ford was a piece of unforgivably bad management. The hill behind him, on which were encamped the Wazamba warriors, seemed to weigh on his neck like a boil. Dr Maine's absurd hat bobbed up and down above the bonnet as he cranked.

Suddenly, it appeared to Charles as though the hat had become even more absurd, that it had, in fact, grown plumes. It bobbed more violently. Dr. Maine's voice came to him curiously distorted, strangled.

'Get away, Charles,' it gasped, with many intervals, 'to the palisade!'

Dr Maine was wrestling with at least one rebellious Wazamba.

Charles, terrified, but with the intention not of running to the palisade but of knocking Dr Maine's assailant severely on the head with the starting handle, crawled laboriously backwards out of the van. As he emerged he felt, with a pang of despair, strong, naked arms seize him, and he smelt the acrid smell of Africans. Twisting round in the powerful grasp, he saw a frightful face, streaked ghastly white, immobile under trembling feathers.

II

At the gate in the palisade the cars halted for not many seconds while the Major arranged with the guards for it to be opened. With this, and in the darkness, and through the concentration on quietness and evasion, the delay of the Ford was not noticed until the other cars were behind the bamboo fence, and Major Brown had jumped out, prepared to rally his forces. At once he went back to the gate, prevented the guards (toothless ex-warriors, long past their prime) from closing it, and strained his eyes against the dark. Nothing could be seen except the vague black masses which were the guest huts. A bird cried twice.

Mr Craig came to the Major's side. 'What on earth has happened to Charles and Maine?' he said, anxiously.

'I must go and see.'

'I shall come, too,' said Mr Craig.

'No. We must have at least one white man here. Just in case there is a slip-up. I'll take William.'

As the Major and William Kapaki walked out, soft-footed, across the open space to the huts, they heard a stifled incoherent cry. Without a word they began to run towards it. Major Brown, as he ran, struggled to get a revolver out of the side pocket of his bush jacket.

The Ford van loomed up in front of them. The front seat was empty. In the back was nothing but the expedition's baggage. William felt something very hard under his bare foot: he bent down and picked up the starting handle.

'*Bwana!*' he whispered, and showed it to Major Brown.

The Major was now very uneasy indeed. With his back to the Ford and his revolver levelled at his hip, he called out: 'Maine, Maine! Where are you?' William stood with the starting handle poised.

There was no answer to the Major's inquiry. A slight breeze, the first of the night, blew gently in his face, and released into the silence a crisp noise from the trees; at the same moment an edge of the moon appeared from the clouds which fringed the sky's borders and cast a faint yellow illumination over the whole scene. The wind passed, and there was no movement anywhere.

Mr Yang and the four warriors of Lugu's who had formed the patrol were already half-way back up the hill, pushing their captives before them. They had, in fact, at one instant, been within twenty yards of the Major and William Kapaki.

III

After a wearisome and fruitless search for Dr Maine and
Charles in all the rooms of the huts, in the other huts round
about, and among the trees, the Major and William returned
to the palisade. Mr Craig was waiting at the gate, pitifully
distracted. His normally quiet and acid manner had vanished
under the strain of his anxiety about Charles: the Major had
almost physically to restrain him from rushing out and taking
on the rebel Wazambas single-handed. The trouble was, as
Mr Craig saw when he became more composed, that nothing
immediately practical could be done about rescuing Charles
and Maine if they had, as seemed certain, been carried off by
the enemy. The forces behind the palisade were not enough
for adequate defence, let alone successful attack. There was a
crumb of comfort in the affair, as the Major pointed out, in
that the abduction had, without doubt, been engineered by
the Count or Yang, and would be used not to harm Maine and
the boy, but for bargaining purposes, if the Count were ever
put again to bargaining. It was hard for the Major to urge Mr
Craig to be patient when his own son stood safely by him, and
he felt something of a hypocrite. But there was no other virtue
worth exercising.

And even as they tried to comfort Mr Craig, and while they
felt the loss of Dr Maine and Charles most keenly, they began
to be involved in pressing but slightly ludicrous events.

The news of their arrival had spread quickly among those
who remained inside the palisade. They were soon surrounded
by old men, women, and children, who gazed at them silently
but beseechingly, like a sick man at a doctor. They, who
seemed at the moment to be losing every round of the fight
against the Count, were relied upon by these people, as gods
are relied on. Into this scene, now lit glitteringly by the moon,
Tetu walked, still wrapped in his blanket, his old eyes
gummy with sleep. He was touchingly pleased to see them,
and proposed to take them straight to Sete's aunt. While he
talked the children squatted, their noses running in the cooler

night air, their faces tilted up to watch what was going on, as though they were at a play.

The Major told Tetu to take his compliments to Sete's aunt and to say that he regretted he could not see her at present as he was, with, he hoped, her consent, arranging the defence of the palace. He then proceeded, as best he could, to make the arrangements.

At intervals round the inside of the bamboo fence were platforms from which, on occasions of war, the defenders of the place could look out on to their enemies and hurl their spears and shoot their bows and arrows at them. The fence itself was stout and still in good repair, but the platforms, having long outgrown their usefulness, had been allowed to get dilapidated. With Tetu as foreman, Major Brown organized gangs of women to make sufficient of the platforms serviceable as to enable a watch to be kept on all sides, and for the riflemen and archers to use as might be necessary. He ordered ramparts to be built on the platforms, of maize-sacks filled with earth: a sack-filling party of children was set to work under Robert's supervision. The palisade gate was guarded by the troops of palsied spearmen, who in spite of their antiquity insisted on putting themselves at the Major's service. On either side of the gate, loopholes were cut in the palisade, and, for those who were to look out of them, breast-high ramparts of earth sacks were constructed. In all these preparations the Major had little faith, though he said nothing.

When the activity set on foot by the Major was at its height, a diversion was caused by the appearance of Sete's aunt on a litter. Four sweating boys struggled under the enormous load. She was dressed as for an important festival; swathed in crimson cloth, on her head a plume of ostrich feathers dyed the same colour, giving her the incongruous appearance of a chaperone at a ball. The tusk of a boar was thrust through an aperture in the flesh which divided her nostrils. Lying beside her on the litter was a huge knife.

She had herself conveyed to where the Major was standing. The boys dropped the litter with somewhat of a bump. With solemnity the Major kissed her hand. With equal solemnity she asked for an explanation of all the work that was going on around her. When she heard the Major's plan of defence, she nodded and said: 'Very good, Brown. The Wazambas will never forget this service. But where is Sete?'

'Where indeed?'

'He is an indifferent general, I imagine,' said Sete's aunt. 'But your preparations are wise and skilful, Brown.'

The Major bowed.

Sete's aunt cackled suddenly. 'And no use.'

The Major looked into the shrewd eyes. 'No use at all, madam,' he said, after a moment's hesitation, 'unless Sete returns quickly.'

Sete's aunt shrugged her upholstered shoulders.

Major Brown said: 'We have discovered that behind Lugu's revolt stands the fat white man who wanted the concession from the Wazambas.'

'So,' said Sete's aunt, unemotionally. 'That comes as no surprise to you and me, Brown.'

'No.'

'And where is Maine and the other boy?'

'Captured by the fat man.'

She made a resonant noise of sympathy. 'We live in bad times, Brown,' she said, and then: 'Well, you must not be kept from important work talking to an old woman.'

She called sharply to the litter boys, lying exhausted on the ground. As they lifted the poles Major Brown pointed to the knife and said: 'Are you going to help in the defence?'

She giggled. 'At my age, and with my size?' She looked away at the mountain snow, glowing a pale, electric blue against the dark sky. 'That, if it becomes necessary, is for me.'

Chapter 17

THE REBELS

I

THEIR mouths and noses still sore from the pressure of the brown hands which had half-smothered them in the frightful journey up the hill, Dr Maine and Charles Craig lay near one of the camp fires. Their hands and feet were rapidly becoming numb from the cords which bound them tightly; as tightly as Mr Yang, revenging himself a little for his skull and his leg, could manage. From time to time smoke blew in their faces, choking them. Ants ran over them, unhindered. The terrifying-looking warriors passed to and fro. No one paid them the least attention.

To Charles, it seemed as though the true nature of life had been suddenly revealed to him. The unpleasantness of his previous life – an injustice done by his mother or father, for example, or a term of struggle with a bully at school – were reduced to mere pin-pricks. Here was something for which feeling sorry for himself could not compensate him, nor did he seem capable of being scientifically detached. Here was a cruel reality which had to be fought against. It would never dissolve of its own accord into the comfortable, kindly existence to which he was used, and which he desired beyond anything else to reassume.

At first he had not been able to see Dr Maine's face: they were back to back. But they had both, with a struggle, turned over, and Dr Maine's first gesture was a great wink which had heartened but not reassured him. Maine's glasses had been lost in the struggle; his eyes looked curiously naked and light without them. No one seemed interested enough to stop them talking, so they had talked, comparing notes about the tightness of their bonds, their squashed noses, their discomfort.

Charles let the question out at last. 'What will they do with us?'

'Not eat us, anyway,' Dr Maine whispered.

Charles laughed nervously: he had already noted the similarity of their predicament to those stories where the victims lie helplessly by a fire on which the cannibals have placed a large cooking-pot.

'Seriously, no need to worry,' went on Dr Maine. 'We are simply hostages, and of all people hostages are taken the most care of.'

'I don't feel I am being taken much care of.'

Dr Maine said: 'Now let us have a quiet half hour of trying to loosen these cords.'

As they struggled, vigorously and painfully, but unobtrusively, they took in, as best they could from their indifferent viewpoint, the details of the rebels' camp. There were not, they estimated, very many warriors, and this confirmed the opinion which the expedition had held all along, that the force which had cut off the way to Makala and surprised Mr Craig and the boys was a small affair, and that Lugu's real strength was held to meet Sete's army somewhere in the north. In apparent charge of the diversionary force was an aged man with a hand missing – clearly not Lugu – and Yang seemed to be acting as a kind of political commissar. There was no sign of the Count. Where was he? Charles asked Dr Maine. With Lugu, the doctor suggested. And the Count's letter? Partly a bluff, perhaps. The occupation of the palace would have only a propaganda value, anyway, with Sete's army still undefeated.

At the end of half an hour the rope round Charles' wrists

was as taut as ever. The skin underneath it was raw. Pretending to wriggle himself into a better position, Charles turned away from Dr Maine, and let fall a few tears of pain and despair. The stars through his moist glasses looked blurred, and he remained with his head averted until they became sharp again.

II

As the night wore on, the rebel warriors began to settle down by the fires, wrapped in their blankets with only their grotesque faces visible. Once, Yang came by, stopped, and looked down on them, seemed about to speak, and then went on. He had a worried look. And then, when Charles, in spite of the pain he was in, was starting to nod, there was a stir in the whole camp as though a wind was blowing through it. In the midst of the bustle the uncertain light from the fires made visible the appearance of a litter borne by four men. When it was lowered, the gigantic form of the Count rolled out of it. A rifle, slung over his shoulder, looked, against his bulk, like a toy. He was wearing a broad-brimmed white felt hat, and smoking a cigar.

Charles never took his eyes off this menacing figure. He could understand now Robert's thorough-going fear of the Count, which hitherto he had been inclined to scoff at. For some time the Count ignored the two captives. He was listening to Yang and the one-handed chief, and speaking occasionally in a voice like the hum of a lethargic insect, but which was reinforced by masterful gestures of the cigar. At last the Count walked over.

Dr Maine said to him: 'Curnow, have this boy untied at once. He is in great pain.'

'Certainly, my dear Maine,' said the Count, astonishingly.

He nodded to Yang, who took out a slim, dangerous knife, and freed Charles' hands and feet. The blood began to flow excruciatingly through the cramped channels. Charles heard himself groan.

The Count said to Dr Maine: 'Your people have moved behind the palisade.'

Dr Maine did not trouble to answer.

'Which means,' the Count continued, 'that my letter is going to be ignored. That is so, isn't it, Maine?'

Dr Maine still did not reply, and the Count smoked in silence for a few seconds, his fat hands very delicately manipulating the cigar. And then the Count's civilized air dropped from him; the graceful hands shook and the voice screeched.

'Isn't it, isn't it?' he cried, kicking Dr Maine several times in the stomach. 'Answer me!'

Dr Maine turned ghastly pale. When he had got back his breath, he said: 'Good gracious, Curnow. Whatever is the matter?'

The Count had by then recovered his suave manner. 'My dear Maine, I am sorry. It is these niggers and this confounded country that made me forget myself for a moment. I cannot, of course, expect you to co-operate with me in the slightest degree, and it was stupid of me to think you might.' With this he walked calmly to one of the other fires.

Charles, appalled, waited for Dr Maine's comment. When it came it was not in the least what he expected.

'What *is* the matter, I wonder?' mused Dr Maine, as though his conversation with Curnow had been of the gentlest.

'With the Count?' said Charles.

'Yes. He usually leaves the brutality to his hirelings. And such temper!'

'Are you all right?' asked Charles. 'Really all right?'

Dr Maine chattered on. 'Perhaps things are not going as well for him as we think. Perhaps Lugu's army has come upon Sete's and been cut about a little.'

'Can't we *do* anything?' said Charles, who was massaging his ankles.

'What?'

'About the attack on the palisade.'

'What?'

'I don't know. But the Major and my father and the others can't possibly defend it against this lot.'

'I place great reliance on Brown's military prowess. I think he'll hold out longer than you think. And I daresay Curnow is not too sure of himself.'

'But what's the point of holding out?'

'There is always a point in holding out. The Count may have fatty degeneration of the heart, and drop dead tomorrow. Or the authorities may have become anxious about your father's absence and sent a company of *askaris*. Or, to be more plausible, Sete and his victorious army may only be a couple of hours away. Don't fret so much.'

Charles could not tell how much of this Dr Maine really meant, or whether he was callous, or merely concealing an anxiety. Charles breathed heavily and the breath escaped as a sigh.

Dr Maine smiled. 'Don't, seriously, worry. Both your father and the Major intend to see this through. Our task is to lie here and not betray them.'

By now one of the warriors was squatting near them, his spear across his bended knees, his motionless face towards them fixed in the wild expression which the paint gave it. He was the guard. Charles became aware that the rest of the warriors were disappearing. He looked round for Count Curnow but the fires were deserted. Soon, an intense stillness settled down on the rebel camp.

'Can't I try to untie you?' whispered Charles to Dr Maine.

Dr Maine shook his head and looked towards the remaining warrior. 'If you tried anything he would stick you through like they stuck that dog through – do you remember?'

Charles remembered. The silence fell again. They both listened, waiting for it to be broken.

III

A similar silence eventually wrapped the palisade. The little boys and girls had filled as many earth bags as they could and had crept away one by one, yawning and rubbing their eyes, to sleep. The platforms were as serviceable as could be expected: on them, on different sides, Robert, Tetu, Mgambe and Mr Craig kept watch. Major Brown went round to them in turn.

He climbed up beside William Kapaki whose side faced the hill which held the rebel encampment.

'Nothing?' asked the Major.

'Nothing, *bwana*,' said William, who was leaning on his ostrich-headed stick, with his rifle propped against the palisade. They both gazed at the hill from which, in three places, came the glow of the rebel fires.

'Joseph understands what is to be done,' said William in an even tone, after a few seconds' silence.

'Yes?' said Major Brown, encouragingly and without the least idea of what William meant.

'Although his eyes look in different directions, nevertheless he can keep a sharp look out,' went on William, after another silence.

Major Brown waited patiently for the point of the conversation to be reached.

William said: 'Joseph could take my place on this platform.'

'Hm,' said the Major. 'And what would you do?'

'I would go,' said William, with a smile that suggested he was asking a rather childish but easily granted favour, 'and look for *Bwana* Maine and the young *Bwana*.'

'Nonsense,' said the Major, decidedly. 'You couldn't help them single-handed. Besides, it is too dangerous.'

The Major knew that neither the Count nor Lugu's men would have the least compunction about William Kapaki, because of his colour. Dr Maine and Charles were safe, though perhaps suffering. William, to the Count, had no hostage or any other value.

But William started again. '*Bwana*, do you think the enemy will wait until dawn, as was stated in the letter?'

'I don't know, William.'

'The enemy knows that we have left the huts and have entered the palisade so as to defend ourselves. He would do better to come while it is still dark. If he comes, *Bwana* Maine and the young *Bwana* will not be so closely guarded.'

'Well?' asked the Major.

'Then I might be able to free them, if you will allow me to go now.'

Major Brown was about to reason with William again when Mr Craig's voice came floating through the dark from the next platform. The Major descended and went to him.

Mr Craig was pacing the platform, sucking a mint lozenge. 'Brown,' he said, 'I am going out to find Charles and Maine. I have thought it over carefully.'

The Major sighed to himself. 'I can't spare you, Craig,' he said. 'You and I and Mgambe are the only decent shots we have. Besides, if you were captured that would be the end of it all.'

'I don't think I care how it ends – whatever "it" may be,' said Mr Craig, in a tired voice. 'What I want is Charles back safely.'

'Can you ensure that by going now?'

'I don't know. I don't know. We have got ourselves into a confounded mess. Maybe, as you say, the best way to make Charles and Maine safe is to defeat the Count – but another way might be to let him win. And another and very obvious way is to rescue them now – and that is what I'm going to try and do.'

'Listen, Craig: if the Count wins he might well cut all our throats – or let Lugu cut them – to stop us blabbing. And if you want to go now, of course I can't stop you. But will you compromise with me?'

'Compromise?'

'Yes,' said the Major. 'William Kapaki has just been trying to persuade me to let him go out to see what he can do for Charles and Maine. I refused, but I'm sure he can do more than you can. I'll let him go, if you will stay.'

'William is a brick,' said Mr Craig, reverting, in his rush of warm feeling, to the slang of his youth, 'but I can't let him take the risk. I must go myself.'

'But he wants to take the risk. And there is much less risk for William – a young, very strong man, from a hunting tribe – than for you, Craig.'

'Can't let him do it. Exceptionally decent of him, but –'

The Major sighed again, and started afresh. 'Look, Craig –' He was resigned to losing one of his force on what he could only regard as a wild goose chase, but he was determined to make it as little of a goose chase as possible. He tried to show Mr Craig the folly of a fifty-year-old white man crawling about Africa in the dark among a rebel tribe.

And in the end it was William Kapaki, a wide grin on his amiable face, who squeezed himself through the palisade gate, opened a fraction by the ancient gatekeepers. Shortly afterwards the silence was broken by a shot from Mgambe's rifle.

Chapter 18

THE ATTACK

I

HE had seen a bunch of white plumes emerge from the trees on the side of the palisade farthest from the hill, and had shot at sight. It was a lucky shot and hit the warrior to whom the feathers belonged just below the heart. He was dead in five minutes.

Count Hugo Curnow was standing among the trees very close to the shot warrior. He heard the shot and saw the result with something like amazement. He had not expected a very effective defence of the palisade. To come up on the wrong side of it, as it were, with the forces at his disposal, seemed to him to be a manoeuvre quite subtle enough to give him the initiative. He knew that there were no effective warriors of Sete's left in the palace, and that there were only two white men.

But Mgambe's shot and the warrior's death had a sensational effect on the Count's men. The one-handed chief, who was at least in nominal command, had been against the attack anyway. He wanted to wait for the arrival of Lugu's main army. The Count, however, had persuaded him that the operation against the palisade would be child's play. The war-

149

riors themselves had been told this. Only four of them could shoot, and these had been armed with some of the Count's rifles. They were less affected than the others at Mgambe's shot; indeed they reacted by furiously blazing away at the dark line of bamboo stakes which was what they saw of the palisade. Their shots whizzed alarmingly but harmlessly round Mgambe, by then crouching behind his rampart of maize bags.

The Count was furious at the shooting: it had given away his position, and if the white men in the palisade had seen the place from which the shots came he might expect more casualties. He ordered One Hand to move the warriors through the trees to the side of the palisade in which the gate was. The warriors moved sullenly, carrying the dead one with them.

Inside the palisade, Major Brown was disposing his forces with care. At Mgambe's shot he had ordered Robert down from his platform.

'Go to the hut where Sete's aunt is – it is about the stoutest – and lie down on the floor until I tell you to get up,' he ruthlessly told Robert.

Robert wailed a protest.

'Quick march!' Major Brown had assumed his fiercest Indian Army manner.

He brought down Mr Craig and stationed him at one of the crude pill-boxes at the side of the palisade gate: he himself manned another. The aged troop of warriors were there, too; very excited and beating their spears on the ground. The Major instructed Mgambe to patrol all the platforms in turn, Tetu and Joseph remaining as look-outs at two of them.

Through his loophole, Major Brown could see the whole length of the street, with the huts on either side. Any attack on the gate must come across the open space which separated it from the town. He waited for the appearance of white plumes, and thought how sad it was that he should have started as student and friend of the Wazambas and ended by killing them. 'Blast Maine and his gold company,' he muttered to himself, stamping his stocky leg.

'What's that?' asked Mr Craig, peeping over his rampart

on the other side of the gate, and looking like an inquisitive rabbit.

'Nothing,' said the Major. 'Talking to myself. Bad habit.'

'I wonder how William is going on.'

'I wonder,' said the Major. Poor Craig, he thought: all this is truly none of his business, and he is suffering the most. I must cheer him up. 'How does this sort of wild-west life suit your digestion?' he called.

Mr Craig groaned facetiously.

The Major fitted the butt of his rifle more comfortably into his shoulder. Here he was; an anthropologist of sorts, the author of two books which had not only sold well but which had caused a little stir in scientific circles: unable to touch his toes any more: long retired from the Army: never heard a shot fired in anger since he was a subaltern – and squinting along an out-of-date rifle with a good chance of getting an up-to-date bullet in his guts. As if Mr Craig had heard his thoughts, the voice of the District Commissioner came floating petulantly over:

'This is really preposterous!'

'I know it is,' said Major Brown. 'I don't quite know how we've got ourselves in this position.'

'*We* haven't done it,' said Mr Craig. 'It is that eccentric and anachronistic figure, Maine. He has everyone playing at pirates with him.'

'He has got to keep his job.'

'He shouldn't be in such a job.'

The silence fell again. Out in the darkness, among the huts, something moved. The short hairs bristled on Major Brown's thick neck: a sensation which brought back suddenly a stream of confused memories of other wars. Almost instinctively he put his two fingers in his mouth and whistled shrilly – the signal to Mgambe. A second after, the dark scene framed by the rectangle of the loophole became swarmingly alive. The air was filled with yellings. The Count's warriors were running towards the gate, holding their spears above their heads like waiters carrying trays.

They were within range at once. It was like shooting at a

fair, thought the Major, as he took aim and fired at their legs. Whatever was the Count thinking of to let his men offer themselves as targets in this way A few seconds after the Major's whistle, Mgambe had joined them at the gate, and was shooting through another loophole. The oncoming warriors began to drop.

In the shadow of one of the huts, Count Curnow bitterly watched them fall. What pitiful material he had to work with! He had not wanted the attack to be precisely like this, but One Hand was responsible for the warriors without rifles: this was the only way they could fight, the way they had fought for centuries. Curnow had ordered his four riflemen, together with himself and Yang, to stay among the cover of the huts and to fire as rapidly as possible at the gate. With the charge of the spearmen thus supported, the Count hoped that the palisade might be carried by brute force, in the first rush. He had reckoned on some rifle fire in return, and on some degree of fortification, but the shooting of the Major, Mr Craig, and Mgambe was deadly, and the earth bags held magnificently. The Count's artillery support seemed to have no effect at all on the return fire. Before the warriors were half-way to the palisade, six of them had fallen, some lying quite still, their painted faces glistening under the moon, others dragging themselves back to the safety of the huts. The remainder began to falter: they remembered the blood of the first man to be hit, gushing blackly from the great hole in his chest. One Hand, who was leading, became more and more convinced of the folly of the fat white man's leadership. He stopped suddenly and shouted hoarsely. The running warriors started to make a wide detour.

As soon as he saw them slanting from the direction of the gate, Major Brown took his finger off the trigger of his rifle. He called to Mr Craig and Mgambe to cease fire. He took a fresh clip, pushed it down and, working the bolt, levered a bullet into the spout; but he knew that the attack had failed, and knew, too, from One Hand's shout, that there might not be another that night.

II

William Kapaki was still within sight of the palisade when he heard Mgambe's first shot. He had stopped, in his laborious crawling through the long grass of the hill, and hesitated, knowing that the attack had started, and wondering if he ought to go back to *Bwana* Brown. But he saw clearly the difficulties of getting back into the palisade. Besides, what he had foreshadowed to the *bwana* had happened; the attack had been made at night. His task of rescuing the young *bwana* and the thin black man should be infinitely lightened. So he pressed on, dragging with him the rifle which Major Brown had told him to bring though he would have much preferred his heavy ostrich-headed stick.

As he crawled, he remembered the stories he had been told as a child by his grandfather. They were about a terrible war in which the old man had fought. 'There may never be a war in your lifetime, little one,' his grandfather used to say, squatting under the poinsettia tree, toothlessly sucking a piece of sugar cane, 'but, if there is, remember this: wars, which we think of as affairs of men in great masses, are in reality composed of hundreds of tiny actions by individual men. Upon the private courage and cunning of the single man depends the result of all wars.' Courage and cunning, said William to himself, toiling on.

Soon he was able to see, although his eyes were so close to the ground, the faint light from the rebel camp fires. He proceeded then without making any noise at all. The fires were in a slight hollow, on the lip of which grew low bushes. Behind the bushes, on a flat ledge of rock, sat the Count's fifth rifleman, his gun across his knees, looking out down the hill, his head-dress merging in the darkness with the outline of the bushes.

Although he had expected a sentry, William could not help drawing in his breath with a hiss when he distinguished suddenly between plumes and foliage. The look-out turned his head towards the noise, but did not otherwise move. William breathed normally again. He decided to go round the look-out: it was stupid to seek trouble by attempting to deal with him. Besides, there might be other look-outs.

With a slowness for which a white man would not have had a tenth enough patience, William began to crawl in a semi-circle round the sentry. Half-way through this tedious progress, he heard very faintly in the distance Major Brown's high whistle to Mgambe, and, immediately afterwards, the rapid detonations from the rifles. Again William felt a pang at having deserted the palisade in its moment of need, but this time he did not stop.

At length he was out of the bushes, and could look down the gentle declivity to where the three fires burned. They were low now, but the middle one was emitting a sufficient glow for him to make out the recumbent figure of Dr Maine, and Charles Craig sitting close by him. A little further away was another plumed warrior. No other figures were visible. This warrior would have to be dealt with; and in a manner which would not make noise enough to draw the look-out down on him. The rifle was useless – for its normal purpose, anyway.

The two captives had a pathetic look. William began to worm his way towards them. He approached the fire from the back of the sitting warrior.

He could not disguise his approach from Charles and Dr Maine: he hoped that they would not, unwittingly, betray him. It was some time, even when he was out of the bushes and into the open, before they noticed him. And then Charles, who was gazing at the night sky, identifying the stars, dropped his eyes. William saw him give a little jump, which he quickly disguised as a sneeze, and then look, in a natural manner, back at the sky. William could even hear what he said to Dr Maine.

'Dr Maine, there is someone coming up behind the sentry. He has a cap on curiously like William Kapaki's.'

Maine's face remained impassive. 'Can't see, myself,' he said. 'Don't do anything, and don't talk more than we have been doing. The sentry is watching us.'

It was oddly unnerving to talk thus openly and not to act in the same way. William slid nearer.

'It is William,' said Charles, in the deadest and most non-committal of voices. 'He's a hero. A trebly-distilled hero. He shall have my six-bladed penknife for this.'

'Steady,' said Dr Maine.

'All right. I shan't give him away. He's got a rifle. And I think he is going to belabour the sentry with it. On the head, probably.'

This was indeed William's plan. He was now six feet away from the still-squatting warrior, and he began very cautiously to lever himself off the ground on to his knees.

The warrior then stood up. Charles felt the blood drain from his face, leaving it prickled. William stayed motionless, in an attitude of prayer. There must have been some slight noise, or something in the faces of the captives, or perhaps a sixth sense, which at that moment gave warning to the sentry that something was seriously wrong, for he whirled round suddenly, his feathers and the tails on his fur cloak flying, and saw William. His long knife was in his hand.

William's reaction was the quicker. He leapt to his feet, and in the same movement brought his rifle butt round in a vicious and rising blow. It caught the sentry in the pit of the stomach, and he fell like a cut tree. But not without first uttering an awful groan which went echoing through the darkness.

'Quick, quick,' said William, running up to Dr Maine. 'There is another warrior on the hill.'

Charles already had his penknife out and was hacking away at the cords on Dr Maine's wrists. William pulled out a knife from a sheath, and set to work at Maine's feet. No one spoke. All were conscious of their danger, but only William knew that the sentry on the hill had a rifle.

Dr Maine's wrists were lacerated by the rope. When he was free he tried to bring his arms from behind his back, and to bend his legs, preparatory to standing. He said: 'It is a stupid thing, but I don't seem able to move my –'

In the middle of this sentence he fell back in a faint. At the

same instant there was the report of a rifle. The other sentry was firing at them.

'Luckily, the Wazambas are bad marksmen,' said William.

Charles felt like a clay pipe in a shooting gallery. 'We must get out of the firelight,' he said.

'Yes, *bwana*,' said William, who was already taking hold of Dr Maine and lifting him.

There was another shot, which ploughed the earth and kicked a shower of embers out of the fire. William seized Maine's thin but lanky body and, half crouching, ran with it into the darkness. Charles picked up William's rifle and followed.

III

Away from the fire, Charles could see on the eastern horizon a thin pale line where it seemed as though the dark night sky were being eased away, like a scab from a scar. This presage of dawn served to remind him that he had not slept all night, and he realized that he was sick with fatigue. His eyes burned dryly, and his stomach felt as though it were divided into a number of empty pockets.

All this positively flashed through his mind: the next instant he was wholly concentrated on Dr Maine's unconscious body, and the shooting which still, now and then, went on.

'Help me to get his head between his knees, William,' he whispered.

They bent Dr Maine over, and a few seconds later felt the limp body quiver. William was very gently massaging Dr Maine's arms and legs with his large, capable hands.

'Must have gone right out,' said Maine, at last, in a small but steady voice. 'Careful with those legs, William; they don't belong to me yet.'

'Can you walk, do you think?' asked Charles. 'They are shooting at us.'

'Only one shooting,' corrected William.

'One is enough,' said Dr Maine. 'Let's try it.'

When he had moved a few painful steps, supported on

either hand by William and Charles, he stopped and said: 'Wait. Where are we going?'

'To the palisade, of course,' said Charles.

'Even though the Count has captured it?'

Charles stared. 'I didn't think of that. And the shooting down there has stopped.' He waited rather stupidly for Dr Maine to say or do something. It seemed to him that they were very perilously poised between two unacceptable alternatives.

'We must go warily,' said Dr Maine. 'We may now have to change our roles, and act the rescuers instead of the rescued.'

'*Bwana*,' said William, 'I will go down to the palisade, and find out what has happened.'

'Will you, my good friend?' said Dr Maine, warmly.

'Yes, *bwana*.'

They continued their tedious progress another three or four hundred yards, deep into the knee-high vegetation on the hillside. Dr Maine gripped William's shoulder.

'Off you go, and good luck,' he said.

Charles slipped the fat penknife into William's hand. In the uncertain light, now turning grey from black, they saw his pleased and charming smile before his agile figure moved out of sight down the hill.

Chapter 19

MORNING

I

NOT far from the palisade, William found himself in the midst of the Count, Yang, One Hand and the warriors returning from the unsuccessful attack. There was little cover: crouching in the grass, a warrior stumbled on him. He dropped his rifle and wriggled away, only to bang into another. He started to make a dash for the palisade. The alarm was raised, the Count saw him, and, drawing a revolver, shot him in the leg as he ran. He was carried back urgently to the rebel encampment, his blood reddening the grass all the way.

When the Count saw that Maine and Charles had escaped, he smiled dreadfully. His naked head was glossy with sweat; his white shorts were grass-stained and dirty; two damp patches extended from his armpits over a large area of his shirt. He affixed his monocle and stared for a full minute at the warrior whom William had clubbed, still lying groaning by the camp fire. The other sentry was explaining wildly to One Hand. Had he not been so desperately short of men the Count would have had them both killed. The spirit of his force was deplorable. Those wounded in the fight at the palisade lay noiseless, with gaunt faces, a ghastly criticism of the attack; spreading a sadness and unwillingness to the un-injured.

'Where are Maine and the boy? How long have they been gone?' he asked William in Swahili. It was an effort for him to speak, to overcome the disgust he felt at the situation; his gorge rose at the thought that he had something to ask of this Negro.

William lay where he had been thrown: his thigh was a confusion of bone and flesh which looked as though it could never be made orderly again. He had glanced at it once, and then away, trying to forget it, hoping it did not belong to him. The Count's questions came to him through a flame of pain which wrapped him round like a coal in a fire. He raised his eyelids, which were turning waxen, and slightly shifted his head. With this movement some large drops of perspiration ran together and started a trickle across his forehead down to the grass.

When he saw William's open eyes, the Count repeated his questions. All around were the squatting or lying warriors: Mr Yang leaned on his rifle, his gold teeth visible in a grin of fatigue. In not one face could William Kapaki see any trace of understanding; from none of these men could he expect any comfort. A giant tear fell out of one eye, and rolled to the ground. He had already forgotten the Count's questions.

The Count walked away from him. The first rays of the rising sun glittered on the monocle wedged among the greyish-white stubble of his unshaven cheeks. He ordered a search to be carried out for the escaped pair by the whole force. He knew how important it might be that day to have his hostages.

Yang put down his rifle, and, overcome by weariness, sank to a squatting posture. 'Lugu will soon be here,' he said soothingly to the Count. 'With his men we can take the pali-sade by weight of numbers. And then it will not matter about Maine and the boy.'

The Count looked down at the little figure, as unreal and ugly as a bad piece of Chinese pottery. Yang was really al-most as stupid as the Negroes. The Count could not bring himself to reply, and walked away before his anger could take charge of him. Yang thought that because Lugu had a few rifles he would necessarily defeat Sete. He had not the imagination to see, as the Count saw, the frightening images everywhere of failure. The litter of the encampment, Kapaki's smashed leg, the morning mists still coiled round the mountain peaks, the palisade in the valley still untaken – all these things tortured the Count's nerves. And he could never forgive himself for his mistake in leaving Lugu and attempting the short-cut to victory via the taking of the palisade. A failure. He should have stayed with Lugu and assured the main victory. He should have known that in war there are no short cuts. Time, time. Pacing this hollow, squalid with the blood and groans of the wounded, he was wasting time. Somewhere else the real events of the war were proceeding, out of his control.

II

Inside the palisade, Mgambe and Joseph had fallen asleep. Major Brown had taken a minute off to go to the hut of Sete's aunt to look at Robert, and had found him asleep, too. He was covered by mats and looked comfortable. The Major glanced up, and through an open doorway saw, in an inner room, Sete's aunt propped up on cushions. She beckoned to him.

'You have driven them off, Brown?' she said.

'For the time being.'

'It is the Gods we have to thank for this.'

'Luck.'

'The same,' said Sete's aunt, with a cackle. 'You know I only say these things because I was brought up to say them.' She took a great draught out of a pot. 'It depends on Sete now, then?'

'Yes.'

'We shall conquer. I foresee it,' she said, making her eyes pop out even more than normally, and staring into space in a prophetic way.

Major Brown was not sure whether she was still joking or not. He said: 'You had my son covered up with the mats?'

Sete's aunt put back her normal face and nodded.

'Thank you,' growled the Major. He grasped her hand and then went back to the gate.

'Still no sign of William?' he said to Mr Craig.

Mr Craig shook his head. His hat was pushed back, showing a face very lined and grey in the morning light. Both men refrained from saying what they thought, that William had been captured by the Count, too.

The Major then went to rouse Joseph, still on his platform.

'What about making us some breakfast, Joseph?'

The platform looked to the north. There was a clear view of some miles over the trees which fringed the river. The mists of the morning were now only ragged wreaths moving across the summits of the mountains. Looking out, the Major saw in the far distance a number of tiny shapes moving towards him. A dust cloud moved with them. He kept them in sight for almost a minute, and then lost them among the undulating ground.

Joseph, by grinning and yawning very briskly, was hoping to make the Major believe that he was already on the way to preparing the meal. 'Before you start on the breakfast,' said the Major to him, 'ask *Bwana* Craig to come here.'

Joseph went off at his fastest pace, a sort of crippled amble, and in due course up came Mr Craig.

'Come and look here, Craig,' said the Major, in a voice of pregnant calm.

Craig wearily ascended to the platform. The moving shapes were visible again, rolling over the country like marbles.

'Lugu,' said Mr Craig, laconically, shading his eyes.

'Or Sete,' said the Major. 'Do you want a little bet?'

'If it is Lugu I shan't be able to collect my winnings.'

Major Brown began to fill his pipe very carefully, as it might have been for his last smoke. 'Well,' he said, 'can you suggest anything we can usefully do?'

'No,' said Mr Craig, turning away and crushing his hat

over his eyes. 'I only wish you had let me go out and look for Charles.'

Major Brown coloured. 'I'm sorry, Craig. Deeply sorry. I did what I thought was best. Come and have some breakfast.'

III

When it had become completely light, Charles and Dr Maine saw that they were in a clump of bushes and cacti which to Charles seemed oddly familiar. He wriggled on further, and found himself looking down on the river at the place of the waterfall and the pool to which he and Robert had gone the evening they had heard Lugu's war-drums. It seemed long ago. But when he had thought a little he realized with a slight shock that it was only the evening before last. As he crawled back to Dr Maine he wondered if the snake was still about which had frightened Robert.

'Yes, I know this place,' he said.

'Can you see the palisade from here?' asked Maine.

'No. But there is a good view across the river. How are your hands and legs now?'

'A deal better.'

'Do you think the palisade will hold out?'

'William will soon come back and tell us.'

'William is a fine fellow,' said Charles, lying on his back, and yawning until his jaw cracked. 'I seem to have done all this before,' he went on, drowsily. 'Looked at the sky here, and felt deadly tired.' He yawned again and then sank right away to sleep.

He dreamed that he was at school and that instead of going to classes he had stayed in bed in the empty dormitory. Out of his half-closed eyes he saw Count Curnow come in at the door: or, rather, although the figure had the Count's physical appearance he knew it to be Robert's headmaster, old Dobbin. Curnow-Dobbin came to his bedside. He pretended to be asleep. The figure had a monocle in each eye; through the glass there was nothing – it was like looking through portholes at sea. 'Craig,' said Curnow-Dobbin, taking him by the arm, 'what have you done with the gold?' The pressure on his arm increased. Still, frightened, he feigned sleep. 'Craig, Craig!'

Charles awoke to find Dr Maine shaking his arm and saying his name in his ear. 'What is it?' he asked, as though he had been awake all the time.

'William has been gone almost an hour,' said Maine.

'That's all right, isn't it? He would have to do the thing cautiously.'

'Perhaps it is all right,' said Maine. 'But I think Curnow's men are looking for us.'

'Oh.'

'Listen.'

There were unmistakable sounds of many men coming the way they themselves had come.

'Shall we find a better hiding-place?' asked Charles. 'Or shall we stick it out here?'

'I think we might try and do better,' said Dr Maine, hastily. 'It doesn't matter about moving so far as William is concerned – he won't try to come back to us while Curnow's men are about.'

'Come on, then,' said Charles. 'If you can manage to get down the slope to the river we'll go behind the waterfall. The river runs over a ledge of rock, and there should be room.'

Dr Maine took a last suck at his cigarette and then stubbed it out. The noises of their enemies grew louder. Stooping double they shambled off towards the river. When they came out of the undergrowth and to the steep slope which fell to the pool, great vistas opened for them to the north. And they saw, far away, the dust cloud and the moving shapes.

'Look!' cried Charles, and then, remembering, lowered his voice to a croak. 'Will it be Sete?'

'Or Lugu,' said Maine. 'The waterfall for us, anyway, whoever it is.'

They felt themselves in a narrowing space between two inexorable forces, like the man in the Poe story. The immensities of Africa seemed suddenly to have shrunk; and they desired to cover themselves completely from view. They scrambled down to the river.

At first there seemed to be no way behind the waterfall. The upper part of the river flowed between its jaw of rock which fell away sheerly to the pool. They had to make a detour from the river to reach its lower part, and there the waterfall appeared isolated on the wall of rock which formed the sides of the pool. They looked up nervously at the heights they had just descended, expecting every instant to see, against the light blue of the morning sky, the feathers of the searching warriors, or the Count's baldness. Charles, though he knew with the rational part of his mind that Lugu's or Sete's men could not be there yet, kept glancing up as well at the other side of the river. As they shuffled precariously round the walls of the rock basin, they imagined themselves already discovered, and the subject of the Count's or Yang's laughter. Everything they did seemed to be futile. They could not hear now whether their pursuers were near: there was no sound but the fall's roaring; and soon they could see nothing but the slippery rock face and the wide column of water moving so rapidly it seemed a solid piece of black-green glass. Their hands, grasping for holds on ferns, disturbed vivid red and blue dragonflies.

IV

The Count's look-outs, which he had posted immediately on returning to camp, brought him the news of the army approaching from the north. He sent scouts out to discover whose army it was, and, preparing for the worst, started planning his retreat. He had his own litter and Yang's and the bearers ready to move off to the cars which were hidden on the far side of the forest. He told One Hand that a reward of a dozen yards of cloth would be given to the man who found Charles and Dr Maine. The search was doubled in speed and intensity.

The Count himself left the camp, and walked a little way up the hill to gaze at the moving figures in the distance on whose identity, it seemed now, the ownership of the gold depended. Mr Yang followed him, a trifle timidly. The Count turned round.

'Stay where you are, you fool,' he said quietly.

Mr Yang showed his teeth in a sickly smile, and went back to One Hand.

The Count looked over the magnificent rolling country, and then looked at his cut and grimy hands. He felt in his pocket for his cigar case, took it out and opened it. It was empty. He remembered now that it had been empty after the attack on the palisade. He scratched the bristles on his cheek, and eased his damp shirt from his body. He thought, for no reason, of his room at Panopoulous' hotel in Mombasa, of the stained plaster walls painted pale blue, of looking out through the grille of the window (sipping at gin and tonic water) into the street below and seeing three Arabs pass, with thick curved daggers in their sashes. And then he thought of the private room in the Johannesburg hotel, panelled in light and hideous wood, where his interviews with McIver of the Consolidated Mining Company always took place. In that room, too, he was smoking and drinking. Such men, Panopoulous and McIver, acute as they were, had no proper conception of reality: no knowledge, really, of life. Even of his, Curnow's, life. The world could be divided into two classes of men – the, so to speak, hotel-dwellers, and the others. The 'others', again, could be divided – the scrupulous and the ruthless. In the end, he told himself, in spite of set-backs, the ruthless 'others' were bound to succeed. It was axiomatic.

With an effort he arrested the flow of images in his mind: he was falling asleep on his feet. He heard some fluty cries behind him, and saw Yang running up the slope.

'They are Sete's warriors,' called Yang, in great alarm. 'The men we sent out are certain. And they have met stragglers from Lugu's army. They think Lugu is dead: he suffered a terrible defeat. Many of his warriors deserted before the battle. The battle was fought at night in a wood. The rifles were almost useless.'

Before this speech was finished, the Count had brushed

past Yang and was on his way to the camp, calling loudly
for his bearers, already, in his imagination, far beyond the
Wazamba frontiers. Yang limped after him. The news of the
defeat spread to the searching warriors. In small groups, bearing the wounded, they vanished into the limitless country.
The two litters plunged into the forest.

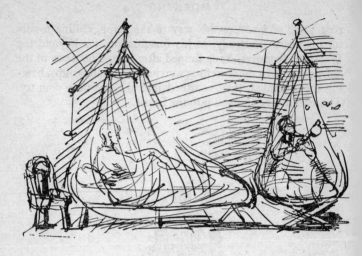

Chapter 20

VICTORY

I

MAJOR BROWN had identified the army when it was still some way off, and with a supreme sense of relief had ordered the gates of the palisade to be thrown open. Soon, the dusty, shouting, excited men were pouring through them. Robert, who not long before had been asleep, could scarcely believe what he saw.

'Is there any news of Charles and Dr Maine?' he asked, putting his lips close to his father's ear to make himself heard through the pandemonium.

The Major shook his head, and went to Mr Craig who was standing watching forlornly.

'Craig, we must ask Sete for some men, and go out at once for Charles and Maine – and William. If they are still in the Count's hands we may be able to cut off his retreat and rescue them.'

Sete was already asking, through the beaming Tetu, for Major Brown. The interview took place in the palace yard:

questions and congratulations were cut short when the Major made his request. Sete expressed his anxiety and gave the Major fifty men to attempt the rescue. His victory seemed to have given him a new benevolence and dignity.

'Please let me come,' begged Robert.

The Major hesitated. 'You can come as far as the camp.'

The rescuers set off up the hill. The sun had become hot, and the sweat poured down the weary faces of the Major and Mr Craig. They walked one on either side of Robert, carrying their rifles, with Sete's warriors spread out around them in an arc.

The hill was utterly quiet: overhead, two vultures sailed. Robert pointed them out, and then, when he saw Mr Craig's expression, wished he hadn't.

The rescuers went cautiously through the bushes which fringed the Count's camp, and then came out over the hollow where there were three blackened patches, once the rebel fires. Around the fires, in the trampled dust, was the litter of the abandoned camp. There, too, lay William Kapaki. Robert saw him first, and instinctively ran towards him down the slope.

'Robert!' shouted the Major. 'Come back!'

Robert returned reluctantly, and the whole party moved forward again at the same careful pace.

'There may be an ambush,' explained the Major. 'Mustn't get separated.'

Robert had eyes for nothing but the figure below in its mauve and yellow jersey. It lay awkwardly and did not move. In a few moments they were up to it.

William was on his back and his eyes were closed. After one look at the wound in his thigh, black with flies, and the huge, dark stain on the grass and the red soil underneath, Robert turned his head away. The thought of William's suffering was unbearable. When the Major bent over him, William opened his eyes.

'It's all right, William,' said the Major in Swahili. 'The rebels have gone away. We have come to rescue you.'

William said one word. 'Finished.'

'No,' said Major Brown. 'I am going to get you better.'

'Finished,' William whispered again.

'Run to the car, Robert,' said the Major, 'and get the first-aid case. Let Joseph run back with it.'

Robert, thankful not to watch, rushed off. Half-way down the hill the image of William's body rose in his mind, and he had to stop.

'He is past the first-aid case,' said Mr Craig.

'I know,' said the Major, his hand over his mouth. 'But there is some morphia in it.'

'I shall never forgive myself for this,' said Mr Craig. '*I* should have that wound. I should have gone out for Charles.'

'It is a wound from a revolver bullet,' said the Major. 'The Count or Yang.'

'Can we ever pin it on them?' said Mr Craig. 'I shall move heaven and earth when we get back to Makala.'

Robert brought the first-aid case back himself. He was exhausted and pale. His father intercepted him as he ran towards William.

'The poor fellow's dead.' The Major's hat was in his hand, and he did not know where to look.

'Oh, Father!' said Robert, turning aside and wanting to run away over the huge green country which lay before him, from the ugly body and the warriors standing silently round it. But it was not until William was lifted and being borne back to the guest huts and he saw the dangling arms and the lightish undersides of the bare feet that the full sense of loss was brought home to him. He started painfully and silently to cry.

II

Mr Craig saw in William's death the dread possibility that Charles had been harmed. When the Major was satisfied that the Count had abandoned the camp, he split the rescuers up into groups, and sent them searching over the hill. Though without a great deal of hope: he thought that Maine and Charles had been carried off, that the Count had still one card up his sleeve. The Major took a dozen warriors and went searching himself: Robert was made to go, too, to take his mind off his unhappiness.

'I can't believe I shall never see William again,' said Robert at last, in a trembling voice. 'Never see him trying to play cricket, or wearing that queer cap.'

The Major was silent. He felt that it was not the Count, nor Maine, nor Craig, who was responsible for his servant's death, but himself. Such senseless fates were always the end of the white man's ambitions and desires. He was filled with a profound disgust for all his activities in the country of the Wazambas.

The Major's group came to the river, and Robert recognized the slope which he and Charles had once climbed. He remembered, too, the strange, uneasy feeling he had had that day, in this place, and William bringing the news of the war. Now there was cause for a deep emotion.

'Charles knows this place – we have been here before,' he told his father. 'Below, there is a pool and a waterfall. Let's look there.'

Very soon Charles and Maine, cramped, exhausted, wet through by the spray from the fall, were discovered in their hide-out. They all shouted for Mr Craig; Charles insisted on grimly climbing the bank to meet him, and was joyfully reunited with his father among the cacti.

The Major silently filled his pipe. When he had lit it he could not help saying to Dr Maine: 'All that remains now is to put William Kapaki in the ground.'

Maine was blinking in the sunlight, a scarecrow figure. 'And get the gold out of it,' he said, quietly.

'Yes,' said the Major. 'The gold. We have all rather lost sight of that.'

'I haven't.' Maine's eyes remained on the Major's.

'We seem to have had many conversations starting like this,' said Major Brown.

'I don't start them. You have the scruples, not I.'

'Haven't you any, then?' asked the Major, brusquely.

Dr Maine turned away. 'You know I have. But I keep them to myself.'

The Major swore, and knocked out his half-smoked pipe savagely. 'Sorry, Maine. I'm a bit on edge. No sleep, and poor William, and my liberal emotions. We have won: Curnow is defeated: Sete is on his throne again: your company has the gold: our futures are assured. We can't have these desirable things for nothing.'

Dr Maine was already walking wearily back to the town. 'You can console yourself with one thing, Brown. The things Curnow wanted would have cost a hell of a sight more.'

The Major said nothing, but wondered. It seemed to him that it was always the well-meaning who were responsible for loss and suffering.

III

The triumphal dance inside the palisade was already beginning as Joseph and Mgambe hacked at the hard soil behind the guest huts. Robert and Charles, sent to bed to be out of the way and to catch up on their sleep, heard the ring of iron with heavy hearts. Charles had told Robert how William had rescued Dr Maine and him, and bravely set off for the palisade, but beyond that they had not spoken. Through the unglazed windows of the hut sounds and voices floated. In the background the drums banged monotonously.

At last the Major called, 'Craig, I've told Joseph to get the Dodge ready for you and the boys first thing in the morning,' and then his cough sounded in the next room as he prepared himself for bed.

Robert raised himself on one elbow, and looked towards the other bed. Charles was asleep, still with his mended glasses on. The window framed a rectangle of sky, growing loose and greenish at the approach of evening. Robert lay back on the canvas cushion which served as a pillow. He was too tired for sleep. Vivid images and fragments of conversation rushed through his mind. He saw a red-plush bucket-chair, an azure menu card with a drawing of a palm tree on it: he saw brown soup rocking gently in a plate with the motion of the ship.

'Can you recommend the soup?' said the charming, slightly foreign voice. 'Can you recommend the soup?'

The day ended as it had begun, with the triviality of the croaking frogs by the river.

STORM AHEAD

Monica Edwards

PS 106

This is a magnificent story of action and suspense. Most of it happens in one weekend – a weekend when time stood still for the Marsh folk, including Rissa and Tamzin, Roger and Meryon (see *The White Riders*). Out of a warm November day when the sun felt like high summer, came disaster – gale, storm, flood. As Jim Decks the ferryman said to Rissa, 'Tidn't nacheral, choose how! Stands to reason you gotter pay for them frolics, see?' They paid. Maroons called out the lifeboat, and everyone in the village came forward to help. In a moment of light Roger saw that 'the tide was high above the highest mark they had ever known it reach before, and the whole sea under the white moonlight was a range of towering, melting mountains, white-topped as any other peaks, but terrifyingly mobile' – and the lifeboat was out in it. The suspense is tremendous, but so truly based that the whole great story reads like something actually experienced and lived through. It is real life, and told with the responsibility felt in any great emergency when all possible help is needed and even children do the right thing as though inspired. Boys and girls (probably over 10 or 11) and grownups will surely enjoy it equally. It would be grand for reading aloud.

THE SECRET OF SMUGGLERS' WOOD

R. J. McGregor

PS 105

Here at last is another mystery story by the author of *The Young Detectives* and *The Secret of Dead Man's Cove*. In it, Dr Douglas, father of Alison, Gordon, and Ian, found a house near the sea, and while the business formalities were going through, he arranged for the children to camp by themselves on the property. The house had stood empty for a long time, and was in the charge of caretakers who were not welcoming. Ian, with his customary curiosity, immediately set the plot in motion, for he found no room to match a window which seemed from the outside just one of the row belonging to the bedrooms facing the front of the house. Then there seemed to be secret understandings between several of the village people; speed boats made mysterious journeys by night, cryptic messages were slipped into coat pockets ... those were some of the clues. The young detectives were sometimes right, sometimes not, but they never let go, and with them, the reader rushes into a thrilling, breathless chase which ends triumphantly. It is a story for boys and girls of 10 to 14.